Jane Eyre

Chosen Classics, Abridged

CHARLOTTE BRONTË

Jane Eyre

**WEBSTER'S WORD POWER
ENGLISH READERS**

With Audiobook, Notes and Glossary

Published 2015 by Geddes & Grosset, an imprint of
The Gresham Publishing Company Ltd,
Academy Park, Building 4000,
Gower Street, Glasgow, G51 1PR, Scotland.

www.geddesandgrosset.com
Contact us at info@geddesandgrosset.com
Find us on 👤 facebook/pages/geddesandgrosset

The publisher acknowledges support from Creative
Scotland towards the publication of this title.

ALBA | CHRUTHACHAIL

ISBN 978 1 910965 17 7

Printed and bound in the EU.

Contents

Introduction   7
  To the Reader   7
  Summary   8
  The Life of Charlotte Brontë   11
  Charlotte Brontë's Life in *Jane Eyre* 14
  The Cowan Bridge Clergy
    Daughters' School   16
  The Narrative   20
  The Main Characters in Charlotte Brontë's
    Jane Eyre   20
  List of Characters   24

Jane Eyre

The Red Room   29
A Man in Black   34
Lowood   40
Red Hair and Curls   46
"Do Not Grieve …"   51
Thornfield   56
The Stranger   63
Mr. Rochester   69
Miss Ingram   76
A Shriek in the Night   81
Teeth Marks   88
A Summer's Night   94
Wedding Day   99

Flight	104
Discovery	108
Ferndean	114
Glossary	123

Introduction

To the Reader

Jane Eyre (published 1847) by Charlotte Brontë (1816–1855) is the story of the life of a young woman, an orphan, who has endured many hardships. She is passionate and emotional, and she has romantic dreams of a better life. However, usually she finds there are barriers in the way of her own happiness and she has to hide her frustrated feelings from the world.

Jane is likeable and moral, and although she is confined by several repressive environments as she grows up, she makes some small acts of rebellion and assertiveness that keep you rooting for her and hoping she will find happiness. It's written entirely from Jane's point of view so we experience all her thoughts and emotions.

This story has been adapted for television, film and theatre many times and once you start reading you'll find out why. It is a very eventful tale, with dramatic (and sometimes tragic) twists, some secrets and lies, and a seemingly impossible romance at its core.

The story has a dark and possibly dangerous male protagonist who Jane quickly falls in love with—Mr Rochester—the epitome of the Victorian romantic hero. Is he in love with Jane too? And what is the secret concealed at his home Thornfield Hall?

In this edition, the story of *Jane Eyre* has been shortened and simplified to make it easier to read. The key characters and storylines are preserved. We also give some historical information about the time and about the author, and provide a glossary of the words and phrases that were common in Victorian times but are unusual now. There is also a summary of the plot that may aid study. Leave this till later if you want the storyline to be a surprise.

If you enjoy this version we recommend that one day you read the whole unabridged tale of Jane Eyre. It is wonderfully written, full of passion and dramatic imagery. A true classic.

Summary

Warning: spoilers! Skip these pages if you want the story to remain a surprise.

This book tells the story of a young woman, Jane Eyre growing up in 19th-century England in the bleak moorland and hills of Yorkshire. The story begins when Jane, an orphan, is ten years old and living with her wealthy but cruel aunt, Mrs. Reed, and her three children, Eliza, John and Georgiana. A servant named Bessie is the only person in the household to show Jane any kindness, telling her stories and singing songs to her. Mrs. Reed's son John is a bully and goes out of his way to frighten and hurt Jane. One day when Jane fights back and attacks John, her aunt imprisons her in the red room, the room in which Jane's Uncle Reed died. While locked in, Jane thinks that she sees her uncle's ghost. Filled with horror she screams and faints from terror. She wakes to find herself in the care of Bessie and a kindly apothecary, Mr. Lloyd, who suggests to Mrs. Reed that Jane be sent away to school. To Jane's delight, Mrs. Reed agrees.

But her delight is short-lived for Jane is sent off to Lowood School where life is hard and far from idyllic. The school's headmaster, Mr. Brocklehurst is a cruel and abusive man who uses the school funds to provide a wealthy lifestyle for his own family while his pupils lead a life of hardship and poverty.

At Lowood, Jane makes her first friend—a young girl named Helen Burns—and for a while she is almost happy. Then typhus sweeps Lowood, and weakened by the typhus, Helen dies of consumption in Jane's arms. The typhus epidemic attracts public attention to the unhealthy and cruel conditions at Lowood and this results in the departure of Mr. Brocklehurst. A group of more sympathetic gentlemen take over the running of the school and Jane's life improves dramatically. She spends eight more years at Lowood, six as a student and two as a teacher.

Jane has known little of the world outside Lowood and yearns for new experiences. She advertises in a newspaper for a post as a governess and gains a position at a large house called Thornfield, where the housekeeper, Mrs. Fairfax, is in charge of the household. Her pupil is a young French girl named Adèle who is the ward of Jane's employer at Thornfield, Mr. Rochester. He is a dark, moody but attractive man and Jane finds herself secretly falling in love with him. She saves Rochester from a fire one night, which he claims was started by a drunken servant named Grace Poole. In another incident, a visitor to the house called Mason is injured by Grace Poole and Jane helps Rochester to care for his wounds before he is sent on his way.

Jane becomes very sad when Rochester brings home a beautiful but unpleasant woman named Blanche Ingram. Jane expects Rochester to propose to Blanche, but instead he proposes to Jane. She accepts and for a month is happier than she has ever been. Mason returns on Jane's wedding day and in the church he cries out that Rochester already has a wife. Mason introduces himself as the brother of that wife—a woman named Bertha. He says that Bertha, whom Rochester married when he was a young man in Jamaica, is still alive. Rochester does not deny Mason's claims, but he explains that Bertha has gone mad. He takes the wedding party back to Thornfield, where they witness Bertha crawling around on all fours and growling like an animal. Rochester has kept Bertha hidden and paid Grace Poole to keep her under control. Knowing that Rochester already has a wife, Jane realizes she can never be married to him and, heartbroken, she leaves Thornfield.

Penniless and hungry, Jane is forced to sleep outdoors and beg for food. At last, she is taken in by three siblings whose names are Mary, Diana and St. John (pronounced

Sinjohn) Rivers, and Jane quickly becomes friends with them. St. John is a clergyman, and he finds Jane a job teaching at a small village school. One day he surprises Jane by declaring that her uncle, John Eyre, has died and left her a large fortune: 20,000 pounds. Jane is amazed when she discovers that her uncle was also St. John's uncle: Jane and her new friends are cousins! Jane immediately decides to share her inheritance equally with her three newfound relatives.

St. John decides to travel to India as a missionary and he asks Jane to come with him as his wife. But as she listens to his proposal Jane hears Rochester's voice calling her name over the moors. Realizing that she cannot abandon forever the man she truly loves, Jane immediately hurries back to Thornfield Hall. She discovers that the house has been burned to the ground by Bertha Mason, who lost her life in the fire. Rochester saved the servants but lost his eyesight and one of his hands. Jane travels to Rochester's new home, Ferndean, and soon Rochester and Jane marry. At the end of her story, Jane writes that she has been happily married for ten blissful years and that Rochester regained sight in one eye and was able to see their first son at his birth.

The Life of Charlotte Brontë

Charlotte Brontë was born on 21 April 1816 in Thornton, a small town just a few miles from the centre of Bradford in the West Riding district of

Yorkshire. She was the third child of Maria and Patrick
Brontë. In all, they had six children: five daughters,
Maria, Elizabeth, Charlotte, Emily and Anne plus a
son, Branwell. Charlotte's father was a clergyman. In
1820 the family moved to the village of Haworth where
the family were to live in the parsonage. In 1821 her
mother died leaving her children to the care of her
husband and her sister, Elizabeth Branwell.

To begin with, Charlotte and her siblings were
educated at home but in August 1824 Patrick
Brontë sent Charlotte, Emily, Maria and Elizabeth
to the Clergy Daughters' School at Cowan Bridge in
Lancashire. Charlotte believed that the poor conditions
they experienced at this school permanently affected
her health and hastened the deaths of Maria and
Elizabeth, who both died of tuberculosis in June
1825. After the deaths of her older sisters, her father
removed Charlotte and Emily from the school much to
their relief. For a few years they enjoyed a daily routine
of lessons, walks and play. With lots of books to study
and enjoy in the parsonage they also wrote their own
imaginary adventures.

However, Charlotte's father was worried that the
time was coming when he would no longer be able to
support his children and he realized that Charlotte
would not be able to help him. Without some formal
education she was unlikely to find a good post as
a teacher or governess in the future. So, from 1831
to 1832 she continued her education as a boarder at
Roe Head School in Mirfield. It was a happy time for

Charlotte. She was soon accepted by the other girls and during her 18 months at Roe Head, she studied hard and improved her skills and knowledge. She came home ready to take on the role of teacher for her sisters.

She returned to Roe Head as a teacher from 1835 to 1838. Then in 1839 she took up the first of many positions as governess to families in Yorkshire, a career she followed until 1841. In 1842 Charlotte and Emily travelled to Belgium to enrol at a boarding school run by Constantin Heger and his wife in Brussels. In return for board and tuition Charlotte taught English and Emily taught music. Their time at the school was cut short when their aunt, Elizabeth Branwell, who had joined the family in Haworth after their mother's death, died in October 1842. Charlotte returned alone to Brussels in January 1843 to take up a teaching post at the school. Her second stay was not happy: she was homesick and in love with Constantin Heger, a married man. She returned home to Haworth in January 1844.

In May 1846 Charlotte, Emily and Anne paid for the publication of a joint collection of poems under their assumed names, Currer, Ellis and Acton Bell. They chose to use these pseudonyms to hide the fact that they were women because at that time women authors were not taken as seriously as male authors. These pseudonyms still used their initials; so Charlotte Brontë was Currer Bell. Their book of poems only sold a few copies and they began to write their first novels.

Charlotte's first book, *The Professor*, did not get published, although she was cheered up by an encouraging response from the publishers, Smith, Elder & Co. of Cornhill. She finished writing *Jane Eyre* and sent them the manuscript for this book in August 1847. Six weeks later *Jane Eyre: An Autobiography* was published. It was a great commercial success and received favourable reviews. In 1848 Charlotte began work on her second novel, *Shirley* but her writing was interrupted when three members of the Brontë family died within a short period: in September 1848, Branwell died of chronic bronchitis made worse by heavy drinking; in December 1848, Emily died of pulmonary tuberculosis and in May 1849, Anne died of the same disease. After Anne's death Charlotte began writing again as a way of dealing with her grief, and *Shirley* was published in October 1849. Charlotte's third novel, *Villette*, appeared in 1853. It was the last of her novels to be published in her lifetime.

In June 1854 Charlotte married Arthur Bell Nicholls, her father's curate, who had been in love with her for a long time. She became pregnant soon after her wedding, but her health deteriorated rapidly. Charlotte Brontë died on 31 March 1855, aged 38, from dehydration and malnourishment due to vomiting caused by severe morning sickness.

Charlotte Brontë's Life in *Jane Eyre*

Many authors borrow experiences from their own lives when they are writing their books. Sometimes this might be a particular place or event that they are familiar with and sometimes the characters in their books may have traits that occurred in people the author has met during his/her own life. In the case of Charlotte Brontë, her books reflect the times she lived in and how they affected her and her family. We are given a picture of life in Yorkshire during her lifetime so not only does her book, *Jane Eyre*, tell the story of a young orphan who eventually finds happiness as a shy young governess but it also tells you what life in general was like for ordinary people during this time.

We are introduced to Jane as a young orphan who has lost her parents at an early age. Charlotte had lost her own mother when she was very young. At this time it was quite common for children to become orphans due to the fact that many adults died at a relatively young age from a variety of illnesses and in childbirth. However, unlike Jane who was sent away as a child because those who should have been caring for her wanted rid of her, Charlotte had a loving family to look after her, including her aunt, Elizabeth Branwell.

Jane's love of books is introduced early in the story and books played a really important part in Charlotte's life. Her home was full of books which were read for pleasure or as part of the Brontë children's home education.

Charlotte describes Lowood School through the eyes of a child (Jane) who is really suffering under its harsh regime and this was something that Charlotte herself experienced as a young child at the Clergy Daughters' School. Charlotte was sent to this school with three of her sisters and their unhappy time there as a result of poor food and harsh discipline was afterwards vividly brought to life in *Jane Eyre*.

While attending the Clergy Daughters' School, Charlotte's two elder sisters both became ill with consumption (tuberculosis) and died shortly after they were removed from the school. The term "consumption" was used because tuberculosis causes the body to waste away or be consumed by the disease. Consumption was widespread in the 19th century and poverty and squalor created the best possible environment for its spread.

In *Jane Eyre*, Jane's friend, Helen Burns, also dies from consumption. The gentle and patient Helen Burns was a reflection of Charlotte's sister Maria. Charlotte later told her editor: "You are right in having faith in the reality of Helen Burns' character: she was real enough: I have exaggerated nothing there."

Like Jane, Charlotte was forced to rely on her intellect in order to achieve economic independence and worked a governess with several different families. Charlotte's own experience as a governess must have informed her description of Jane's experiences at Thornfield as Adèle's governess. It was common for children to be educated at home with the help of a governess and teaching, either in a private house or in a private school, was regarded as suitable employment for young middle-class ladies whose families were no longer able to support them.

When you read the story of *Jane Eyre* you can be

sure that Jane's experiences are a reflection of some of Charlotte's own life experiences but remember that it is Charlotte's skills as a writer that make her tale so enjoyable.

The Cowan Bridge Clergy Daughters' School

In England, there was no national system of education for boys and girls before 1870 and any schools that did exist were set up by wealthy local benefactors or people who saw it as a means of making a living. In the early 19th century many more boys and girls were educated in schools run by religious or philanthropic groups. Some of these were run as private schools and some as so-called "Charity Schools".

As workers migrated into the cities in search of work in the factories of the Industrial Revolution, living conditions for many in these urban areas were very basic, and cheap child labour was common. Charity schools were mainly concerned to educate such impoverished children in the knowledge and practice of Christianity and to prepare them for apprenticeships or domestic service.

Middle-class children were increasingly being sent as boarders to small private schools, where the living conditions were extremely basic and cruel punishments were common. Some, like Lowood School in *Jane Eyre* were set up by clergymen to educate the daughters of poor clergymen, often for employment as governesses.

The school that served as the model for Lowood School in Jane Eyre was Cowan Bridge Clergy Daughters' School, a school intended for the daughters of financially disadvantaged clergymen. It was founded in 1823 by the Reverend Carus Wilson and was first located in the village of Cowan Bridge in the English county of Lancashire, where it was attended by the Brontë sisters. The age of the pupils varied from six years to twenty-two years. Two of the sisters, Maria and Elizabeth, died of tuberculosis after attending the school for only a short time.

The fees were half those of other similar schools which was welcome news for Charlotte's father who was poorly paid as a clergyman. However the welfare of his daughters was very important to him and the decision to send them away to school as boarders was not an easy one.

The school sat in an isolated position on the lower slopes of Leck Fell and, depending on the season it was often hidden in low-lying mist, torrential rain or snow blizzards. A row of stone cottages housed the teacher's quarters, the kitchen, dining room and some small bedrooms. An old mill stood at right angles to the cottages and it had been converted into the schoolroom with the main dormitory above it, and opposite this was a long, covered walkway where the girls could exercise in bad weather.

The girls had to wear a special school uniform that unfortunately labelled them as "charity children"—something Charlotte hated—but they also had to come with a large amount of other clothing including "four day shirts" and "three white upper petticoats".

Most of the girls slept two to a bed in the single large dormitory above the schoolroom. The strict and harsh regime followed by the girls at Cowan Bridge was more or less as described in the chapter on Lowood in *Jane Eyre*. They were given a "plain and useful education" with the goal of achieving "intellectual and religious improvement" (as stated in an advertisement of the time for the school). Personal cleanliness, neatness and discipline were expected of every child. Punishments at the school ranged from wearing badges for being untidy to beatings in front of the whole school.

The hardest days for the children were the Sundays. In all weather and without adequate protective clothing, the pupils had to walk more than three miles (five kilometres) across the fields to their pastor's church to attend the first service. They were given a cold snack at the back of the church before having to endure endless services before finally returning to their school. On arriving, back at the school, cold and famished, they were given a whole slice of bread, spread with rancid butter. Their Sunday devotions were not finished yet and ended with long recitings of the catechism, learning long biblical texts by heart, and hearing a sermon of which the theme was often about eternal damnation.

However, as far as the pupils were concerned by far the greatest hardship they had to endure was the food or lack of it. The food was badly prepared and so poor that many of the pupils couldn't eat it and this contributed significantly to their ill-health. The many illnesses experienced by pupils at the school, such as typhus and consumption, were sadly very common in the life of a child at boarding school in the 19th century. Many seriously ill pupils had to be sent home where they died shortly afterwards.

Free compulsory education for all children in the UK came into being after the 1870 Education Act.

The Narrative

This book is written like an autobiography. It is a first-person narrative which means it is written from the point of view of one person. Narrative is another word for a story or a written account of something. In a first-person narrative you'll read: "I thought", "I suffered", "They were kind to me." In this kind of narrative you see the events through one person's eyes. We only get their side of the story. The first-person narrative is a good way to make us really empathize with Jane Eyre.

In the original novel, *Jane Eyre*, Charlotte Brontë often uses the phrase, "Dear reader"—another way that Jane can create a bond with the reader while narrating her life story. In this adapted edition, John Kennett has cut out all of these references. While the tone of Jane's voice has been kept throughout very effectively, we wish to point out to you that he cut one of English literature's most famous lines, namely "Reader, I married him", which Jane uses to explain that she has finally achieved her dream and got married to Mr. Rochester.

The Main Characters in Charlotte Brontë's *Jane Eyre*

Warning: spoilers! Skip the rest of the Introduction if you want the story to remain a surprise.

Jane Eyre

Jane Eyre is the main character and narrator of the book. She is an intelligent, modest, plain-looking young girl who becomes a passionate and strongly principled woman. Jane values freedom and independence and from her childhood on she battles to find her own place in a society that regarded women as second-class citizens. An orphan from an early age, she has to contend with bullying, inequality, and hardship throughout her childhood but she always succeeds in asserting herself. When she agrees to marry Mr. Rochester it is not because she wants to make a good marriage and take her place in society but because she genuinely loves him. However, when she discovers that Rochester is already married she refuses to stay with him. Their marriage some years later is all the sweeter for Jane knowing she did not sacrifice her moral principles but retained her dignity and self-respect.

Mrs. Fairfax

Mrs. Fairfax is an elderly widow and the housekeeper of Thornfield Hall. She is kind to Jane from the moment they meet, making her feel welcome and always ready to give her good advice on social matters. She runs the household very efficiently for Mr. Rochester who is happy to leave her to look after his home and his ward, Adèle. Jane likes and respects her and turns to her when she is frightened or unsure of herself. Mrs. Fairfax is a kind and caring but rather one-sided character, as we only see her from Jane's perspective. It is not clear if she knows that Bertha Mason, the mad woman looked after by Grace Poole, is in fact Mr. Rochester's first wife. She tells Jane that Mr. Rochester has "family troubles" which would imply that she knows that Bertha Mason is a relative (but not necessarily his wife). At the same time she would probably not have approved of Jane's marriage to Rochester if she had known that he was already married to another woman.

Mr. Rochester

Charlotte Brontë has created Edward Fairfax Rochester as a Byronic hero (a type of literary character named after the English poet Lord Byron [1788–1824]). The Byronic hero is usually dark and moody, very intense, mysterious, emotional, troubled and arrogant. Mr. Rochester is all of these things and like other literary heroes of the day he is a rich, dashing and romantic character.

A wealthy man with a large home, Thornfield Hall,

he is the only man that Jane is eventually able to meet as an equal (after she gets her inheritance and refuses to be his mistress). This, despite their difference in backgrounds and social status. His great passion and forcefulness make him extremely appealing to Jane. Nevertheless, he is also a complicated man and far from perfect, treating Jane and Adèle at times with disdain and cruelly making Jane jealous by pretending he is going to marry Blanche Ingram.

In the end, Mr. Rochester shows great courage when he tries to save his mad wife from the fire that destroys Thornfield Hall and leaves him blind. When he and Jane finally meet again, his love for her is unchanged and he humbly begs her to marry him.

St. John Rivers

St. John (pronounced Sinjohn) Rivers and his two sisters take Jane in at Moor House after she has run away from Thornfield Hall and Mr. Rochester. They turn out to be Jane's cousins. St. John is a clergyman and a very devoted Christian. He is a very different sort of man to Mr. Rochester. A serious and reserved man, he has a much colder personality than Mr. Rochester who is full of passion and emotion. He does try to help Jane and finds her a job as a teacher at a girls' school in a nearby village. But some time later he plans to travel to India as a missionary and he asks Jane to accompany him as his wife. He is not in love with Jane but sees her as the sort of woman who would make a good missionary's wife. Her response to his request is to immediately think of Rochester and how much he meant to her and she to him. The next morning she is gone and St. John is left to go to India on his own.

List of Characters

JANE EYRE, the main character and narrator of this book

MR. JOHN REED, Jane's maternal uncle

MRS. SARAH REED, wife of Dr. Reed and Jane's aunt by marriage

JOHN REED, Jane's cousin

ELIZA REED, Jane's cousin

GEORGIANA REED, Jane's cousin

BESSIE LEE, a nursemaid at Gateshead

ABBOT, a maid at Gateshead

DR. LLOYD, the man who recommends that Jane be sent to school

MR. BROCKLEHURST, the clergyman, director and treasurer of Lowood School

MISS MARIA TEMPLE, the kind superintendent of Lowood School

MISS MILLER, a teacher at Lowood School

HELEN BURNS, Jane's best friend at Lowood School

EDWARD FAIRFAX ROCHESTER, the master of Thornfield Hall

PILOT, Mr. Rochester's dog

ADÈLE VARENS, Mr. Rochester's ward to whom Jane is governess

SOPHIE, French nurse to Adèle Varens

MRS. ALICE FAIRFAX, an elderly and kindly widow and the housekeeper of Thornfield Hall

LEAH, the housemaid at Thornfield Hall

JOHN, an old, and normally the only, manservant at Thornfield

MARY, John's wife, the cook

BERTHA ANTOINETTA MASON, Mr. Rochester's wife

GRACE POOLE, Bertha Mason's caretaker

BLANCHE INGRAM, a socialite whom Mr. Rochester courts for a short while to make Jane jealous

COLONEL DENT, a friend of Mr. Rochester

SIR GEORGE LYNN, a friend of Mr. Rochester

RICHARD MASON, an Englishman from the West Indies, the brother of Bertha Mason

MR. CARTER, a surgeon who looks after the injured Mason

MR. BRIGGS, the solicitor of Jane's uncle, John Eyre

ST. JOHN RIVERS, a clergyman who befriends Jane and turns out to be her cousin

DIANA and MARY RIVERS, St. John's sisters and Jane's cousins

REVEREND WOOD, clergyman

Jane Eyre

Chapter One

The Red Room

We did not take a walk that day because of the rain and the cold winter wind. I was glad of that. I never liked long walks on chilly afternoons.

After dinner the three Reed children—Eliza, John and Georgiana—sat with their mother in the drawing-room. I slipped away into the room next door and found myself a book, a big, heavy one, all about British birds. I curled up in the window seat and drew the curtains close behind me.

I read happily for some time. And then I heard the door open.

"Boo!" cried the voice of John Reed.

I kept still and quiet. I was afraid of John Reed. He bullied me all the time and my flesh shrank when he came near me. He was a schoolboy of fourteen, and I was a girl of ten. He was tall and stout for his age, while I was small and thin, with eyes too big for my face. He ate too much and had flabby cheeks, and he hated me because his mother was not my mother and he did not think it right for me to live in her house. She was my aunt, and the house was called Gateshead. She never saw John strike me: he always did it behind her back.

I could feel him there, on the other side of the curtains, frowning at the empty room.

"Where the dickens is she?" I heard him say. "Lizzy, Jane's not here. Go and tell mother she's run out into the rain. She'll get into trouble for that."

He sounded pleased. Then Lizzy spoke.

"She's in the window seat, I expect."

I came out hurriedly, before John had a chance to drag me out.

"What do you want?" I asked breathlessly.

"Say 'Master Reed' when you speak to me," was the answer. "Now, come here!"

He dropped into an armchair and waved for me to stand before him. I came up to his chair. He put out his tongue at me as far as it would go. In a moment, I knew, he would strike me. I waited. He said nothing, but hit out suddenly and strongly. I tottered and almost fell. He'd hurt me and I bit my lip to stop myself from crying.

"That's because I don't like the look of you," he sneered.

I said nothing. I just watched him, knowing that he would hit me again.

"What were you doing behind the curtains?" he asked.

"I was reading."

"Show me the book."

I went over to the window and got it.

"You've no right to take our books," he said. "You have no money; your father left you none; you ought to be a beggar and not live here with gentlemen's children like us. My mother has to give you food and clothes, when you don't belong here. Now, give me that book and go and stand by the door!"

I went to the door and turned. I saw him stand and lift the book, ready to throw it. I started aside with a cry of alarm, but I was too late. The book hit me and I fell, striking my head against the door and cutting it. I felt blood running through my hair and the pain was so sharp that I forgot all my terror.

"You cruel boy!" I gasped. "You're like a murderer—"

"What!" he cried. "I'll pay you back for that!"

He ran at me. I felt him grasp my hair and my shoulder. At that moment I really saw him as a murderer. I felt a drop or two of blood from my head trickle down my neck. I turned on him in a fury, tearing and scratching with my hands. He roared out loud.

"Rat! Rat!"

Lizzy screamed and ran for Mrs. Reed. She came running into the room, followed by Bessie and Abbott, the maid. We were parted. Mrs. Reed, I saw, was white with anger.

"Take her upstairs," she said between her teeth. "Take her away to the red room and lock her in there."

Four hands were laid on me and I was dragged upstairs. I fought all the way, which was a silly thing to do because it made Bessie and Abbott angry with me.

"She's like a mad cat!" gasped Bessie as they dragged me into the red room. "Now, Miss Eyre, sit down and think over your wickedness!"

They thrust me upon a stool. I rose from it like a spring. Their hands grabbed me again.

"If you don't sit still," Bessie threatened, "you'll have to be tied down."

I knew by the look on her face that she meant what she said. I sat still. Miss Abbott folded her arms and looked at me darkly.

"Say your prayers, Miss Eyre," she said, "or else something bad might come down the chimney and carry you away."

They went out. I heard the lock click. I was alone.

The red room was never slept in after Mr. Reed died there. There was a big bed in it, with curtains of deep red; the carpet was red, and the table at the foot of the bed was covered with a crimson cloth; the blinds were drawn down over the two large windows.

The room was chill and silent. I was not quite sure whether they had locked the door, and when I dared move I got up and went to see. Yes! I was shut in until they chose to let me out.

I went back to my stool, and sat thinking about my troubles. Why could I never please? Why was I always suffering? I tried so hard to please Mrs. Reed. I did all that she asked me, and yet I was called naughty and tiresome, sullen and sneaking, from morning to night.

My head still ached and bled. I sat in that quiet room a long, long time and cried my heart out. Daylight began to fade. It was past four o'clock and the grey afternoon turned to twilight. The rain beat on the windows and the wind howled around the house. I grew as cold as stone and my spirits sank within me. I began to think about Mr. Reed, who had died in this very room nine years before. I could not remember him, but I knew that he had been my mother's brother and that he had taken me into his own house and promised my mother that he would look after me as one of his own children.

If my uncle had been alive, I thought, he would have treated me kindly. Then I remembered that I had heard that dead men came back from the grave to punish people who did not keep their promises; and I was sure that my aunt stood in need of punishment. I thought that Mr. Reed's ghost might return and rise before me in this room.

It was a frightening thought. I tried to put the idea from my head. I wiped my tears and hushed my sobs, afraid that my grief might cause a ghostly voice to comfort me, or that I might see, in the gloom, a ghostly face bending over me with strange pity. I lifted my head and tried to look boldly round the dark room.

What was that?

I saw something gleaming against the wall. Was it a beam of moonlight shining through the blind? No! Moonlight was still, and this light moved, gliding up to the ceiling and quivering over my head. I was suddenly filled with horror. My heart beat quicker, my head grew hot. A sound filled my ears, like the rushing of wings. Something seemed near me. I could not breathe. I rushed to the door and shook it, trying to get out. I began to scream and scream.

Chapter Two

A Man in Black

My screams changed to sobs when I heard steps running along the outer passage. The key turned. Bessie and Abbott entered.

"Miss Eyre, are you ill?" cried Bessie, white-faced.

"Take me out!" I begged. "Put me in the nursery!"

"What for? Are you hurt?" Bessie demanded.

I clutched her hand.

"I saw a light, and I thought a ghost would come," I stammered.

"What is all this?"

It was my aunt's voice. She came along the passage, her gown rustling stormily.

"I gave orders that Jane Eyre should be locked in the red room till I let her out myself," she snapped.

"Miss Jane screamed so loud, ma'am," pleaded Bessie.

"Let go of her hand," was the answer. "Jane Eyre, you will now stay here an hour longer, and I will only let you out then if you have been still and quiet."

"Let me be punished some other way!" I begged. "I shall be killed if—"

"Silence!" cried Mrs. Reed, and she thrust me back into the room.

The door slammed shut, and the key turned in the lock. I heard the rustle of her gown as she swept away.

I stared all round the dark room, filled with fright and terror. Then I fainted and darkness closed the scene.

The next thing I remember is waking up with a feeling as if I had had a frightful nightmare. I opened my eyes and knew that I was in my own bed in the nursery. It was night, for a candle burnt on the table. Bessie stood at the foot of the bed, and a man sat in a chair near my pillow, leaning over me. I knew him: it was Doctor Lloyd.

I spoke his name and put out my hand. He took it, smiling and saying, "We shall do very well by-and-by."

He patted my hand, drew Bessie aside and spoke to her quietly. When he left the room, Bessie came to my bedside.

"Bessie, what's the matter with me?" I asked. "Am I ill?"

"You were sick with fright, I should think," said Bessie kindly. "The coachman went across the lawn with a lantern, and you must have thought the light was a ghost. You'll be all right in the morning."

Next day, by noon, I was up and dressed, and sat wrapped in a shawl by the nursery fire. Bessie was there with me. All the Reeds were out driving in the carriage. Before they returned Dr. Lloyd came again.

"Well, nurse, how is she?" he asked, as he entered the nursery.

Bessie answered that I was doing very well.

"Then she ought to look more cheerful. You've been crying, Miss Jane Eyre. Can you tell me what about? Have you any pain?"

"I'm crying because I am miserable."

The doctor looked puzzled. He stared at me for a long time, then said:

"What made you ill yesterday?"

"I was shut up in a dark room where there is a ghost."

I saw Dr. Lloyd smile and frown at the same time.

"Ghost!" he said. "You are afraid of ghosts?"

"Of Mr. Reed's ghost I am. He died in that room. It was cruel to shut me up without a candle. I shall never forget it."

"And is that what makes you so miserable?"

"No. I am unhappy, very unhappy, for other things."

"What other things?"

"For one thing I have no father or mother—and John Reed says that I have less right here than a servant. If I had anywhere else to go, I should leave this place. I hate living here!"

Dr. Lloyd smiled at me in a kind way.

"Would you like to go to school?" he said.

I thought about that. I scarcely knew what school was, but if it took me away from the Reeds it would be the beginning of a new life.

"I should indeed like to go to school," I said.

At the same moment the carriage was heard rolling up the gravel walk. Dr. Lloyd got to his feet.

"Well, who knows what may happen?" he said to me, then, turning to Bessie: "Is that your mistress, nurse? I'd like to speak to her before I go."

After that I hoped and prayed that I should be sent away to school. Days and weeks passed and my aunt never spoke of it, though I felt sure she would not keep me much longer under the same roof with her. I felt, all the time, that she could hardly bear to look at me. John often put his tongue out at me, but kept away from me after I had flown at him like a mad cat.

Christmas came. For the Reed children there were presents, dinners and evening parties, but I was left out of every enjoyment. I sat in the nursery and listened to the sound of the piano below, or crept to the head of the stairs and peeped at the passing to and fro of the butler and footman, carrying in the trays of refreshments.

And then, on the fifteenth of January, about nine o'clock in the morning, I was sitting on the window-seat of the nursery, breathing on the frost-flowers with which the glass was covered. I could see the porter's lodge and the carriage-drive and I saw the gates thrown open and a carriage roll through. I watched it sweep along the drive, and stop in front of the house. The doorbell rang loudly and the newcomer was admitted. All this meant nothing to me, but in a few minutes Bessie came running upstairs.

"Miss Jane, take off your pinafore," she cried. "Have you washed your hands and face this morning?"

I nodded. She passed a bristly brush over my hair and pulled off my pinafore. She then hurried me to the top of the stairs and told me to go down at once to the breakfast room.

I went down slowly. Who could want me, I wondered? I was more than a little frightened. I stood in the empty hall, afraid and trembling, for some minutes. The ringing of the breakfast room bell confirmed that I must go in.

I walked slowly to the door. The handle turned, the door unclosed, I passed through and curtseyed. I looked up. Mrs. Reed was sitting by the fireside, and a man was standing on the rug. He was dressed in black from head to foot, and seemed as tall as a tree. His grim face was like a carved mask. His eyes were grey, under a pair of bushy brows.

Mrs. Reed waved a hand at me.

"This is the little girl," she said.

"Her size is small," said the man in a deep voice. "How old is she?"

"Ten years."

"What is your name, little girl?"

"Jane Eyre, sir."

"Well, Jane Eyre, are you a good child?"

I was silent. Mrs. Reed shook her head sadly and said:

"The less we say about that the better, Mr. Brocklehurst."

"I'm sorry to hear it," said the man gravely, and he sat down in the armchair opposite Mrs. Reed's. "Come here," he said to me.

I stepped across the rug. He placed me square and straight before him. What a face he had, now that it was on a level with mine! What a great nose! What a mouth!—and what large teeth stuck out of it!

"So you're a naughty girl, are you?" he said. "Do you know where the wicked go after death?"

"They go to hell," I answered.

"And what must you do if you don't wish to go there?"

I thought a moment and then answered:

"I must keep in good health and not die."

"Children younger than you die every day," he replied grimly. "Do you read your bible?"

"Sometimes."

"And the psalms? I hope you like them?"

"No, sir. Psalms are not interesting," I remarked.

"Oh, shocking!" he said, rolling up his eyes. "That proves you have a wicked heart."

"I told you that, Mr. Brocklehurst," said my aunt, "in the letter I wrote you three weeks ago. If you take her into Lowood School, I should be glad if your teachers were asked to keep a strict eye on her."

My heart missed a beat. For the next minute I heard no more. My only thought was that, at last, I was to be sent away to start a new life in a new place. I was glad, at that moment. But then, I had no idea of what lay ahead. If I had known, I should not have felt so pleased.

Chapter Three

Lowood

Not one of the Reeds said goodbye to me when I left. It was soon after five on the morning of the 19th of January that I rose and made myself ready. The moon was set, and it was very dark. I was to leave by a coach which passed the lodge gates at six a.m.

Bessie walked with me along the drive. Raw and chill was the winter morning, and the cold set my teeth chattering in my head. A light was showing in the porter's lodge. My trunk, which had been carried down the evening before, stood corded at the door, the porter's wife waiting beside it.

A minute or two later I heard the distant roll of wheels. I went to the gate and watched the coach lamps approach rapidly through the gloom.

The coach drew up. My trunk was hoisted on top, and I threw my arms round Bessie's neck.

"Be sure and take good care of her," she cried to the guard as he lifted me inside.

"Ay, ay!" was the answer.

The door was slammed and on we drove.

I remember but little of the journey: I only know that the day seemed very long. The afternoon came on wet and misty and, as it waned into dusk, I began to feel that we were getting very far indeed from Gateshead.

When twilight came I dropped asleep. The coach had stopped when I awoke. Its door was open and a person like a servant was standing at it. I saw her face and dress by the light of the lamps.

"Is there a little girl called Jane Eyre here?" she asked.

I answered, "Yes", and was then lifted out; my trunk was handed down and the coach drove away.

I looked about me. Rain, wind and darkness filled the air, but I saw a wall before me and a door open in it. Through this door I passed with my new guide, who shut and locked it behind her. Before me was a big house with many windows, in some of which a light was burning. We entered a door and the servant led me through a passage into a room with a fire, where she left me alone.

I stood for some minutes, warming my numbed fingers over the blaze, then the door opened and two ladies entered. The first was a tall lady with dark hair, dark eyes, and a pale face. She looked at me for a moment or two, then said:

"The child is very young. She had better be put to bed soon. Let her have some supper before she goes to bed, Miss Miller." Then she touched my cheek gently and added: "I hope you will be a good child, Jane Eyre."

Miss Miller led me from the room. We passed through passage after passage, till we heard the hum of many voices and entered a wide, long room, with great pine tables, and seated all round on benches a large number of girls of every age from nine to twenty. They were all dressed in brown frocks and long white pinafores. It was the hour of study and they were all looking over their tomorrow's task.

Miss Miller signed to me to sit on a bench near the door. Then she ordered the lesson books to be collected. When that had been done, she said:

"Monitors, fetch the supper trays."

Four tall girls went out, and came back in a minute or two, each bearing a tray. I was handed a mug of water and some pieces of thin oatcake. I drank for I was thirsty, but was so tired that I did not touch the food.

The meal over, prayers were read by Miss Miller, and the classes filed off, two and two, upstairs. I was by now so tired that I hardly noticed what sort of a place the bedroom was. Miss Miller helped me to undress. When laid down I looked at the long rows of beds, each of which held two girls. The light was put out, and I fell asleep.

When I again opened my eyes a loud bell was ringing. Day had not yet begun to dawn, and a candle or two burnt in the room. The girls were up and dressing. I, too, rose and dressed in the bitter cold and washed in a hand basin. Again the bell rang. We all formed in line, went down the stairs and entered the cold and dimly lit schoolroom. Prayers were read by Miss Miller and the first lesson began.

It went on till day had dawned, when the bell sounded again. Once more we formed a line and marched into another room for breakfast. How glad I was at the thought of getting something to eat! I was now nearly sick from hunger, having eaten so little the day before.

On all the tables in the low-ceilinged dining-room smoked basins of something hot. To my dismay, however, it smelled far from inviting. A long grace was said, a hymn sung, and then we all sat down. A plate of porridge was set before me. I ate a spoonful or two without thinking of its taste, and then suddenly knew that it was badly burnt. It was horrible stuff. The spoons were moving slowly. I saw each girl taste her food and try to swallow it, but most of them wrinkled their noses and gave up. Breakfast was over—and none had breakfasted. Thanks were returned for what we had not got, a second hymn chanted, and we all went back to the schoolroom.

A quarter of an hour passed before lessons began again, during which time we were allowed to talk freely. All the talk was about the miserable breakfast we had been served.

A clock in the schoolroom struck nine. Miss Miller entered and cried:

"Silence! To your seats!"

We began to work in groups. After some minutes the lady I had seen the night before entered the schoolroom and began to teach the bigger girls. She was, I was told in a whisper, Miss Temple, the superintendent of Lowood.

It seemed a long morning, but at last the clock struck twelve. The superintendent rose.

"I have something to say to you all," she said. "You had this morning a breakfast which you could not eat, so you must be hungry. I have ordered that a lunch of bread and cheese should be served to all."

Both pupils and teachers looked at her with a sort of glad surprise. She left the room and in a little while the bread and cheese was brought in and given out, to the high delight of the whole school. When we had eaten the order was given: "To the garden!" We each put on a straw bonnet and grey cloak and, following the stream of chattering girls, I made my way into the open air.

As yet I had hardly spoken to anyone, and nobody seemed to take any notice of me. I stood lonely enough, drawing my cloak around me and trying to forget the cold which nipped me. The sound of a cough close behind made me turn my head. I saw a girl sitting on a stone bench nearby. She was bent over a book, but then looked up and said:

"I suppose you are an orphan?"

"Yes," I said, "my parents died before I can remember."

"All the girls here have lost either one or both parents."

"Does this house belong to the tall lady who said we were to have some bread and cheese?" I asked.

"To Miss Temple? Oh, no! I wish it did. She has to answer to Mr. Brocklehurst for all she does. He buys all our food and clothes."

"Does he live here?"

"No—two miles off, at a large mansion."

"Do you like the teachers?"

"Well enough."

"Have you been here long?"

"Two years."

"Are you happy here?"

"You ask too many questions, and I've answered enough for the moment. Now I want to read."

But at that moment the bell rang and we all went back to the schoolroom. Lessons went on till five o'clock, but the only thing I can remember about that afternoon was that I saw the girl with whom I had talked in the garden sent to stand in the middle of the large schoolroom as a punishment. I wondered what sort of girl she was, whether good or naughty.

Soon after five o'clock we had another meal—a small mug of coffee and half a slice of brown bread. I ate and drank with relish. I could have eaten three times as much, for I was still hungry.

Half an hour's play followed, then study; then the glass of water and the piece of oatcake, prayers, and bed.

Such was my first day at Lowood Orphanage.

Chapter Four

Red Hair and Curls

My first two or three months at Lowood seemed an age. During January, February, and part of March, all the countryside lay under deep snow and we suffered much from the cold. We had no boots, the snow got into our shoes and melted there; our ungloved hands became numbed and covered with chilblains, as were our feet. All the time we were given only the barest amount of food to keep us alive.

One afternoon, as I was sitting with a slate in my hand, puzzling over a sum in long division, I lifted my eyes to the window and caught sight of a figure just passing. It was Mr. Brocklehurst, looking longer and narrower than ever.

Two minutes later, all the school rose to their feet and Mr. Brocklehurst entered. He stood at Miss Temple's side, and as I happened to be seated at the front of the room I caught most of what he said:

"I was surprised, Miss Temple, when settling accounts with the housekeeper, to find that a lunch of bread and cheese has been twice served out to the girls during the past fortnight. Why is this? We have never given them lunch before. Whose idea was it?"

"Mine, sir," replied Miss Temple. "The breakfast

was so badly cooked that the pupils could not eat it. I couldn't let them go hungry until dinner-time."

Mr. Brocklehurst looked shocked at this.

"Madam," he said sternly, "you must know that my plan in bringing up these girls is not to overfeed their vile bodies, but to make them patient, hardy and self-denying."

He paused and looked round the schoolroom. Suddenly his eyes gave a blink and his face took on a shocked look once more.

"Miss Temple," he demanded, "what—what is that girl with curled hair? Red hair, ma'am, curled—curled all over?"

He raised his cane and pointed to the awful object, his hand shaking as he did so.

"It is Julia Severn," replied Miss Temple, very quietly.

"Why has she curled hair? You know I cannot have that!"

"Julia's hair curls naturally," returned Miss Temple still more quietly.

"Naturally! What has that to do with it? I have said again and again that I want the hair of these girls to be cut close and arranged modestly. I will send a barber tomorrow, for I see others who have far too much hair. Tell all the first form to stand and turn their faces to the wall."

Miss Temple gave the order. All the biggest girls obeyed, though I could see them pulling faces when their backs were turned to Mr. Brocklehurst. He looked at the head of each in turn, while we all waited in breathless silence. His words sounded like a death sentence:

"All those topknots must be cut off!"

Miss Temple opened her mouth to speak, but Mr. Brocklehurst raised a hand.

"Madam," he said, "I will have no argument on this. Each of these girls has a string of hair in plaits. That, madam, is vanity! They must be cut off—"

He stopped short. Three other visitors, ladies, now entered the room. All were finely dressed in velvet, silks and furs; all had long, curled hair; all were members of Mr. Brocklehurst's family, the girl next to me whispered.

Mr. Brocklehurst turned and bowed to them. At the same moment my slate slipped from my hand and fell with a crash. Every eye in the room was turned upon me, as I stooped to pick up the broken pieces.

"A careless girl!" cried Mr. Brocklehurst. "Ah, it is Jane Eyre, I see. Well, I have something to say about her. Come here, Miss Eyre!"

I was so frightened that I could not move. Two of the big girls, however, tugged me to my feet and pushed me forward.

"Fetch that stool," said Mr. Brocklehurst, pointing to a very high one.

It was brought forward.

"Place the child upon it."

I was placed on the stool, by whom I don't know. Mr. Brocklehurst stood beside me.

"Ladies," he said, turning to his family, "Miss Temple, teachers, and children—you all see this girl?"

Of course they did! I could feel their eyes scorching my skin.

"You see that she is young. It is my sad duty to warn you that this girl is also wicked. I have been told so by her aunt. You must be on your guard against her. Have nothing to do with her. Do not speak to her and do not let her take part in your games. Teachers, you must watch her, for this girl is—a liar!"

"How shocking!" I heard one of the ladies whisper.

"Her aunt has sent her here to be healed of her sins," Mr. Brocklehurst went on. "I beg all of you to see that it is done."

He turned away. His family moved towards the door. Mr. Brocklehurst turned and looked back.

"Let her stand half an hour longer on that stool," he said, "and let no one speak to her for the rest of the day."

The door closed behind him. I stood there, burning with shame. Long minutes passed, and then a girl came up and walked by me. It was Helen Burns, the girl with whom I had talked in the garden. In passing she lifted her eyes and smiled. When she returned to her place, she smiled at me again as she went by. What a smile! I remember it now, and how it seemed to give me strength. I knew, in that moment, that I had found a friend.

Before the half-hour ended, five o'clock struck. The girls went off for tea. I now dared to get down from the stool. It was deep dusk. I crept into a corner, sat down on the floor and began to sob. I wished that I were dead, then started up—again Helen Burns was near me. She came up the long room, bringing my coffee and bread.

"Come, eat something," she said.

I went on weeping aloud, feeling as if a drop or a crumb would choke me. She sat down beside me, hugged her knees with her arms, and stayed completely silent. I was the first to speak:

"Helen, why do you stay with a girl whom everyone believes to be a liar?"

"Jane, you are wrong. Most of us feel very sorry for you. Mr. Brocklehurst isn't liked here. Besides Jane—" she paused.

"Well, Helen?" I said, putting my hand into hers.

"I'll be your friend," she said simply.

I put my head on her shoulder and my arm round her waist. She drew me near to her, and we sat in silence.

I would not then have exchanged Lowood, with all its hardships, for Gateshead and its daily luxuries. For the first time in my life I had found a friend.

Chapter Five

"Do Not Grieve ..."

As the weeks passed Lowood came to seem a better and brighter place. Spring drew on, and flowers peeped out amongst the leaves of the garden. On Thursday afternoons (half-holidays) Helen and I took walks, and found still sweeter flowers opening by the wayside, under the hedges.

Lowood itself lay in a wooded valley that was the cradle of dank fog—and the fog brought sickness, which, with the coming of spring, crept into the orphanage and breathed typhus through its crowded schoolroom and dormitory. Before the coming of May the school had been turned into a hospital.

Lack of food, and neglected colds, had left most of the pupils very weak: forty-five out of the eighty girls lay ill at one time. Classes were broken up and we were given more freedom. Those girls who were lucky to have friends and relations willing to take them in were sent home. Many, already ill, went home only to die. Some died at the school and were buried quietly and quickly.

Death, then, became an inhabitant of Lowood. But while there was gloom and fear behind its walls and rooms and passages steamed with hospital smells, the bright May sunshine fell on the bold hills and beautiful woodland out of doors. Those of us who stayed well enjoyed the beauties of the scene to the full. We were allowed to ramble in the woods like Gipsies from morning till night. We did what we liked, went where we liked, and enjoyed ourselves thoroughly.

Then Helen Burns fell ill and was shut away in some room upstairs. She was not in the hospital part of the house, for her complaint was consumption, not typhus, which I thought was something mild that time and care would cure.

Once or twice, on very warm afternoons, she came downstairs and sat in the garden; but I was not allowed to go and speak to her.

One evening, at the beginning of June, I stayed out very late with a girl called Mary Ann Wilson. We'd wandered far and lost our way, and it was after moonrise when we got back. A horse, which we knew to be the doctor's, was standing at the garden door.

"Someone must be very ill," said Mary Ann sadly, "if they've sent for Doctor Bates at this time of the evening."

She went into the house. I stayed behind a few minutes to plant in my garden a handful of roots I had dug up in the forest. I heard the front door open. Doctor Bates came out, and with him was a nurse. After she had seen him mount his horse and ride away, she was about to close the door, but I ran up to her.

"How is Helen Burns?" I asked.

"Very poorly," was the answer. "The doctor says she'll not be here much longer."

I knew at once what she meant. Helen Burns was living her last days in this world. I felt a strong shock of horror, then a thrill of grief, then a wish to see her. I asked in what room she lay.

"She is in Miss Temple's room," said the nurse.

"May I go up and speak to her?"

"Oh, no, child! Now it's time for you to come in. You'll catch the fever if you stop out when the dew is falling."

I went in. It was nine o'clock and Miss Miller was calling the pupils to go to bed.

I could not sleep that night. Some hours later I rose softly from my bed, put on my frock over my night dress, crept from the dormitory and set off to find Miss Temple's room. I knew that I must see Helen to give her one last kiss before she died.

I found Miss Temple's room. A light shone through the keyhole and under the door. Everything was still and quiet. I opened the door and looked in.

Close by Miss Temple's bed, and half covered with its white curtains, there stood a little crib. I saw the outline of a form under the clothes, but the face was hidden by the hangings. The nurse to whom I had spoken in the garden sat in an easy chair, asleep. I crept towards the crib. My hand was on the curtain, when I paused, afraid that I had come too late and might find death.

"Helen," I whispered softly, "are you awake?"

She stirred herself, put back the curtain, and I saw her face, all thin and pale.

"Is it you, Jane?" she whispered.

"Oh!" I thought, "she is not going to die. They are mistaken. She could not speak so calmly if she were."

I got on to her crib and kissed her. Her forehead was cold, and her cheek cold and thin, as were her hand and wrist; but she smiled as of old.

"Why are you here, Jane?" she asked.

"I came to see you. I heard you were ill and I could not sleep till I had spoken to you."

"You came to say good-bye, then. You are just in time."

"Are you going somewhere, Helen? Are you going home?"

"Yes, to my long home—my last home."

"No, no, Helen—" I began.

I stopped. While I tried to hide my tears, a fit of coughing seized Helen. It did not, however, wake the nurse. When it was over she lay some minutes as if quite worn out. Then she whispered:

"Jane, your feet are bare. Lie down and cover yourself with my quilt."

I did so. She put her arm over me and I nestled close to her. After a long silence she whispered:

"I'm very happy, Jane. When you hear that I am dead, you must be sure not to grieve. We all must die one day, and I have no pain."

I clasped my arms closer round her. She seemed dearer to me than ever. I felt as if I could not let her go. Presently she said:

"How comfortable I am! That last fit of coughing has

tired me a little. I feel as if I could sleep. Don't leave me, Jane. I like to have you near me."

"I'll stay with you, Helen. No one shall take me away."

"Are you warm?"

"Yes."

"Good-night, Jane."

"Good-night, Helen."

She kissed me, and I her. We both soon slept.

When I awoke it was day. I seemed to be moving. I looked up. I was in somebody's arms. The nurse held me and was carrying me back to the dormitory.

Later, I learned that Miss Temple, who had been tending a sick pupil, came back to her room at dawn and found me lying in the crib, my face against Helen Burns' shoulder, my arms around her neck. I was asleep, and Helen was—dead.

Her grave is in Brocklebridge churchyard. For fifteen years after her death it was covered only by a grassy mound. Now a grey marble headstone marks the spot, and on it is her name.

I had it put there.

Chapter Six

Thornfield

After the fever had killed more than thirty of the girls, it gradually disappeared from Lowood. When, however, the number of its victims became known, public attention was drawn to the school. Why, it was asked, had so many young girls died in that one spot? Certain facts became known: the site was unhealthy; the girls were poorly fed and clothed; the water was impure—all these things were discovered.

Several wealthy people in the neighbourhood gave money towards the building of a better school in a more healthy spot. In time, we moved to this new place, were given better food and clothing, and the orphanage became a far finer place than the old one. I lived eight years behind its walls, six as a pupil, and two as a teacher. During these eight years my life was not unhappy, but at the end of that time it altered.

Miss Temple, who had been a good friend to me, married a clergyman, moved to a distant country, and was lost to me.

From the day she left it was no longer the same. That very evening, I remember, I went to my window, opened it, and looked out. Beyond the grounds of the school I could see a white road winding far away. How I longed to follow it further! For eight years I had known little of the outer world. All my holidays had been spent at school, and my aunt had never even written to me. I wanted suddenly to be in a new place, amongst new faces, in a new house ... .

But how did people get to a new place? I had no answer.

Then, as I lay sleepless in my bed that night, the answer came to my mind. I would advertise in a newspaper for a post as a teacher or governess.

I was up at first light. An hour later I had my advertisement written and addressed to the county newspaper. I posted it after tea.

The next week seemed long. Then an answer came—a letter sealed with the initial F. I broke it. The contents were brief.

"If J. E., who advertised in the —shire Herald of last Thursday, is in a position to give satisfactory references as to character and ability, a situation can be offered her where there is but one pupil, a little girl, under ten years of age; and where the salary is thirty pounds a year. J. E. is asked to send references, name, address, and all particulars to Mrs. Fairfax, Thornfield Hall, near Millcote, ——shire."

The writing was like that of an old-fashioned and elderly lady. Mrs. Fairfax! I saw her in a black gown and widow's cap. Thornfield Hall! It sounded very fine and grand. Millcote, I knew, was a large town, and I longed to go where there was life and movement.

Within a few days I sent off references signed by the inspectors and superintendent of the school. I waited anxiously for a reply from Mrs. Fairfax. It came. I was to take up the post of governess in two weeks' time; and two weeks later, indeed, I sat in the coach which was to take me to new duties and a new life at Thornfield.

I had been told that when the coach stopped at the George Inn in Millcote, there would be someone to meet me. It was dark when we arrived, and I looked anxiously around for someone to speak my name and for the carriage that would carry me to the house. There was no one there.

I asked to be shown into a private room, and here I waited, filled with all sorts of fears and doubts. At last a waiter came into the room.

"Is your name Eyre, miss?" he asked.

"Yes."

"Person here waiting for you."

I jumped up and hurried into the passage. A man was standing by the open street door and beyond him I dimly saw a one-horse carriage. The man pointed to my trunk in the passage.

"This'll be your luggage, I suppose," he said.

"Yes."

He hoisted it onto the coach and I got in. He shut the door behind me and we drove off through the misty night.

It was more than an hour later when the driver got down and opened a pair of gates. We passed through and they clashed shut behind us. We followed a drive and came upon the long front of a house. Candlelight gleamed from one window only. The coach stopped at the front door. It was opened by a maidservant. I got out and went into the house and the maid led me across a square hall with high doors all round. She knocked on a door and ushered me into a snug, small room where a cheerful fire burned. A little, elderly lady was sitting in an armchair beside it. She wore a widow's cap, a black silk gown, a snowy apron, and was busy knitting.

"How do you do, my dear?" she said. "You must be cold and tired. Come to the fire."

"Mrs. Fairfax?" I asked.

"Yes, my dear. Do sit down."

I sat and she ordered the maid to bring me a tray of food.

"Shall I see your daughter tonight, Mrs. Fairfax?" I asked.

"My daughter!" she said, surprised. "Oh, you mean Miss Varens. Varens is the name of the little girl you are to teach."

"Indeed! Then she is not your daughter?"

"No, I have no family. Little Adèle Varens only came here last autumn. It's funny how the child has made this old house come alive; and now you are here I shall be quite happy."

She smiled pleasantly and my heart warmed to her.

"I won't keep you up talking tonight," she went on. "It's nearly midnight and you must be tired. I'll show you your room. I've had the room next to mine made ready for you."

She led me to a fine, large bedroom. The door closed

behind her, and I felt a sudden sense of safety. I was soon in bed and asleep. When I awoke it was broad day.

I rose; I dressed myself with care; I went down the oak staircase into the hall. The house was very fine and grand, and the hall door stood open. I went out onto the lawn and studied the front of the mansion. It was three storeys high, and its grey front stood out well from the background of a rookery and, farther off, wooded and lonely hills.

Mrs. Fairfax appeared at the front door.

"What! Out already?" she said, and smiled. "How do you like Thornfield?"

"Very much indeed."

"Yes," she said, "it's a pretty place. I fear it will be getting out of order unless Mr. Rochester uses it more often."

"Mr. Rochester!" I exclaimed. "Who is he?"

"The owner of Thornfield," she answered. "I am only the housekeeper."

"And the little girl, my pupil?"

"She is Mr. Rochester's ward. He asked me to find a governess for her. And here she comes, with her nurse."

I turned and saw a little girl come running up the lawn. She was about eight years old, slight and pale, with thick fair hair falling in curls to her waist.

"Good morning, Miss Adèle," said Mrs. Fairfax. "Come and speak to the lady who is to teach you."

The little girl turned at once to her nurse and spoke rapidly in French. I stared.

"Are they foreigners?" I asked.

"The nurse is a foreigner, and Adèle was born on the Continent. She speaks both French and English, but you'll understand her in either, I dare say."

Luckily I had been taught French at Lowood. I shook hands with the girl and spoke to her in her own tongue. She was a little shy at first, but after we were seated at the breakfast table she made friends and soon chattered all the time.

After breakfast, Adèle and I went into the library, which was to be used as a schoolroom. And there, as pupil and teacher, we passed a pleasant enough morning. When noon came I sent her off to her nurse. As I climbed the stairs to my own room Mrs. Fairfax called to me from the hall. She asked me if I would like to see over the rest of the house. I gladly agreed and followed her upstairs and downstairs, admiring as I went, for all was well arranged and handsome. The bedrooms at the top of the house I thought especially grand, and I liked the hush and dimness of the rooms in the day.

"Do the servants sleep up here?" I asked.

"No, they sleep at the back. No one ever sleeps here. If there were a ghost at Thornfield Hall this would be its haunt."

I smiled.

"You have no ghost, then?"

"None that I ever heard of," answered Mrs. Fairfax, smiling back at me.

She took me up a very narrow staircase to the attics and then by a ladder and through a trap-door to the roof of the hall. Leaning over the battlements, and looking far down, I saw all the grounds laid out like a map. It was a bright and pleasant scene. When I turned away from it and re-passed the trap-door, I could scarcely see my way down the ladder. The attic seemed as black as a vault.

Mrs. Fairfax stayed behind a moment to fasten the trap-door. I groped my way out of the attic and went down the narrow garret staircase. I waited in a long, dim passage, with its two rows of black doors all shut, like a corridor in some Bluebeard's castle.

As I paced softly on, the last sound I expected to hear in so quiet a place struck my ear. It was a curious laugh, very clear but low and mirthless. I stopped. The sound ceased for an instant, then began again, this time much louder. It passed off in a mad shriek that seemed to wake an echo in every lonely room.

There was dead silence for a second or two while I stared wide-eyed into the gloom, and a thin, cold trickle seemed to creep through my heart. Mrs. Fairfax had said that all these rooms were empty; that Thornfield had no ghost; but I could have pointed out the door through which the sounds had come.

Chapter Seven

The Stranger

There was a quick step on the stair behind me. I turned and saw Mrs. Fairfax sweeping towards me.

"Mrs. Fairfax!" I called. "Did you hear that loud laugh? Who is it?"

"Some of the servants, very likely," she answered. "Perhaps Grace Poole. She sews in one of these rooms. Sometimes Leah is with her. They are often noisy together."

The laugh sounded again, dying away in an odd murmur.

"Grace!" exclaimed Mrs. Fairfax.

I did not expect anyone to answer, for the laugh was as ghostly as any I had ever heard; but the door nearest me opened, and a servant came out—a woman of between thirty and forty, red-haired and with a hard, plain face.

"Too much noise, Grace," said Mrs. Fairfax. "Remember what I have told you!"

Grace curtseyed silently and went in. I followed Mrs. Fairfax downstairs and we found dinner ready and waiting for us in her room.

Several times, during the next few weeks, I heard Grace Poole's strange laugh. I heard, too, her odd murmurs, even stranger than the laugh. There were days when she was quite silent, but there were others when I could not account for the odd sounds she made. Sometimes I saw her. She would come down from her room with a basin or tray, go to the kitchen, and shortly return with a pot of ale in her hand.

October, November, December passed away. I grew to like my pupil, and to feel towards Mrs. Fairfax a thankfulness for her kindness.

One afternoon in January Mrs. Fairfax begged a holiday for Adèle, who had a cold. I agreed that this was wise and, since I was tired of sitting still in the library through a whole long morning, I put on my bonnet and cloak and set out to walk two miles to the village of Hay, with a letter that Mrs. Fairfax wished to have posted.

The ground was hard, the air freezing. It was three o'clock, and the sun already low in the sky. Far and wide on each side there were only fields, and all the countryside lay sunk in a deep sleep. I loved the peace of it all and, when I was half-way to the village, I sat down on a stile which led into a field. With my cloak gathered about me, and my hands in my muff, I did not feel the cold, though it froze keenly, as was proved by a sheet of ice covering the lane just below the point where I sat. I stayed there till the sun went down amongst the trees, and sank crimson and clear behind them. Then I dropped down from the stile and turned on my way.

I'd taken no more than three steps when I heard a ringing of hoofs along the road. A horse was coming, though the windings of the lane hid it from my sight. As the path was narrow, I went back to the stile and waited for the horse to pass.

On the hill-top above me sat the rising moon. The horse was near, but not yet in sight, when I heard a rush under the hedge and a great black and white dog came gliding along the lane. I drew back in fright, but he passed me quietly enough. The horse followed—a tall steed, and on its back a rider. He was, I thought, a traveller taking the short cut to Millcote. He passed and I went on; a few steps and I turned: a sliding sound, a cry, and a clattering tumble had arrested my attention. Man and horse were down; they had slipped on the sheet of ice which glazed the lane. The dog came bounding back and barked till the evening hills echoed the sound. He snuffed around his master and then ran up to me. I walked down to the traveller, who was by this time struggling free of his steed.

"Quiet, Pilot!" he said to the dog.

"You must just stand on one side," he said as he rose, first to his knees, and then to his feet. I did, whereupon he helped the horse heave itself to its feet, with much stamping and clattering of hoofs. The traveller felt his foot and leg, then limped painfully to the stile and sat down.

"If you are hurt and want help, sir, I can fetch someone from Thornfield Hall or from Hay," I offered.

"Thank you, I shall do. I have no broken bones— only a sprain."

He stood up and tried his foot.

"Ugh!" he said, and I saw his face twist with pain.

The moon was bright and I could make him out plainly. He wore a long riding cloak, fur collared and steel clasped. He was of middle height, but very big in the chest. He had a dark face, with heavy eyebrows, and was about thirty-five years of age. I felt no fear of him, and no shyness, though he frowned at me and his voice was deep and harsh.

"Where do you come from?" he asked.

"From Thornfield, the house with the battlements just below. I am going to Hay to post a letter, and will get help for you if you wish it."

"Whose house is Thornfield?" he asked.

"Mr. Rochester's."

"Do you know Mr. Rochester?"

"No, I have never seen him."

"You are not a servant at the Hall, of course. You are—" He stopped and ran his eye over my dress, frowning.

"I am the governess."

"Ah, the governess!" he repeated; "devil take me. I had forgotten the governess!"

He rose from the stile. His face twisted with pain when he tried to move.

"You may help me, if you will be so kind," he said. "Try to get hold of my horse's bridle and lead him to me. You are not afraid?"

I shook my head and went up to the tall horse. I tried to catch the bridle, but the horse was a spirited thing and would not let me come near it. I tried again and again. The traveller waited and watched, and at last he laughed.

"I must beg of you to come here," he said.

I came.

"Excuse me," he said, "but I am forced to make use of you as a walking-stick."

He laid a heavy hand on my shoulder and, leaning on me with some stress, limped to his horse. Having caught the bridle, he sprang to his saddle, pulling a face as he made the effort.

"Thank you," he said to me. "Now make haste with your letter, and return as fast as you can."

The touch of a spurred heel made his horse rear and then bound away; the dog rushed after them; all three vanished.

I took up my muff and walked on. I was annoyed with myself because I could not forget the picture of his face that had been imprinted on my mind. It was a dark, strong face, and I had it still before me when I entered Hay and slipped the letter into the post-office. I saw it yet as I walked fast downhill all the way home.

I went into the hall and caught the sound of Adèle chattering cheerfully. I hastened to Mrs. Fairfax's room. A fire was burning, but there was no candle; and no Mrs. Fairfax. Instead, all alone, sitting upright on the rug, I saw a great black and white long-haired dog. He got up and came to me, wagging his tail. I rang the bell, for I wanted a candle. Leah entered.

"What dog is this?" I asked.

"He came with master."

"With whom?"

"With master—Mr. Rochester. He is just arrived."

"Indeed!"

"Mrs. Fairfax and Miss Adèle are with him in the dining-room, and John is gone for a surgeon. Master had an accident. His horse fell in Hay Lane, and his ankle is sprained."

"Oh!" I said. "Bring me a candle, will you, Leah?"

Leah brought a candle immediately. She entered, followed by Mrs. Fairfax, who said that Mr. Carter, the surgeon, had arrived, and was now with Mr. Rochester. Then she hurried out to give orders about tea, and I went upstairs to take off my things.

Chapter Eight

Mr. Rochester

Mr. Rochester went to bed early that night; nor did he rise soon next morning. When he did come down it was to attend to business in the library.

Adèle and I had now to move into a room upstairs. Adèle was not easy to teach that day. She kept running to the door and looking over the banisters to see if she could catch a glimpse of Mr. Rochester.

We dined as usual in Mrs. Fairfax's parlour. The afternoon was wild and snowy, and we passed it in the schoolroom. When dusk came I allowed Adèle to put away her books, and to run downstairs. I sat by the schoolroom fire until Mrs. Fairfax came in.

"Mr. Rochester would be glad if you and your pupil would take tea with him in the drawing-room at six o'clock," she said. "You'd better change your frock now. I'll come with you and fasten it. I always dress for the evening when Mr. Rochester is here."

I went to my room and put on my second-best dress of black silk, and a little pearl brooch which Miss Temple had given me as a parting gift. Mrs. Fairfax then took me down to the drawing-room.

Two wax candles stood lighted on the table, and two on the mantelpiece. Basking in the light and heat of a great fire lay the dog, Pilot, with Adèle kneeling near him. Half lying on a couch was Mr. Rochester, the fire shining full on his face. I knew my traveller with his thick eyebrows, and the sweep of his black hair. He never lifted his head as we drew near.

"Here is Miss Eyre, sir," said Mrs. Fairfax.

He bowed, still not taking his eyes from the group of the dog and child.

"Let Miss Eyre be seated," he said.

I sat down. I felt interested to see how he would go on. He sat like a statue, neither moving nor speaking for some minutes, while Mrs. Fairfax talked in her pleasant way.

"Madam, I should like some tea," was the only answer she got.

The tray was brought in. I went to the table with Adèle, but the master did not leave his couch.

"Will you hand Mr. Rochester's cup?" said Mrs. Fairfax to me.

I did as she asked. He looked up at me as he took the cup from my hand.

"I have examined Adèle and find you have taken great pains with her," he said. "She has made much improvement."

"Sir," I said, "I am obliged to you."

"Humph!" said Mr. Rochester, and he took his tea in silence. We heard no more from him until the tray was taken away, when he turned to us and said: "Come to the fire."

We obeyed. Adèle was ordered to amuse herself with

Pilot, while Mrs. Fairfax got on with her knitting. Mr. Rochester looked at me.

"You have lived in my house three months, Miss Eyre?"

"Yes, sir."

"And you came from—?"

He paused. I told him that I was an orphan and that I had come from Lowood.

"Humph!" he said, when I had done. "Last night in Hay Lane you made me think of fairy tales. I half believe you bewitched my horse. Who advised you to come here?"

"I advertised and Mrs. Fairfax wrote to me."

"Yes," said that good lady, "and I am very glad that I did. Miss Eyre has been a wonderful companion and a kind and careful teacher to Adèle."

"Don't trouble yourself to give her a character," returned Mr. Rochester. "I shall judge for myself. She began by felling my horse."

"Sir?" said Mrs. Fairfax, looking bewildered.

He smiled.

"What did you learn at Lowood?" he asked me. "Can you play?"

"A little."

"Go into the library. Take a candle with you and leave the door open. Sit down at the piano and play a tune."

I rose and obeyed.

"Enough!" he called out in a few minutes. "You play a little, I see, like any other English schoolgirl. Adèle showed me some sketches this morning which she said

71

were yours. Fetch me your portfolio so that I may see them."

I brought the portfolio from the library. He looked at each sketch and painting. Three he laid aside; the others he swept from him.

"Take them off to the other table, Mrs. Fairfax," he said, "and look at them with Adèle. You," glancing at me, "sit down and answer my questions. When did you find time to do these? They have taken much time and some thought."

"I did them in the last two holidays I spent at Lowood."

"Where did you get your copies?"

"Out of my head."

"That head I see on your shoulders?"

"Yes, sir."

"Has it more of the same kind within?"

"It may have: I should hope—better."

He spread the pictures before him and looked at them for a long time.

"They are good," he said at last. "There—put them away."

I had scarce tied the strings of the portfolio, when, looking at his watch, he said abruptly:

"It is nine o'clock. What are you about, Miss Eyre, to let Adèle sit up so long? Take her to bed."

Adèle went to kiss him before leaving.

"I wish you all goodnight," he said, and made a movement of his hand towards the door as if he were tired of our company.

I saw Adèle to bed, and went down to Mrs. Fairfax's room.

"Mr. Rochester is very changeful and abrupt," I remarked.

"True," said Mrs. Fairfax, "but he has painful thoughts to worry him."

"What about?"

"Family troubles," she answered vaguely. "He's not often here, you know. He'll go away soon."

"Why doesn't he like Thornfield?"

"Perhaps he thinks it gloomy."

She would say nothing more on the subject, and it was clear that she did not wish me to make her. Mr. Rochester remained something of a mystery to me.

For the next few days I saw little of him. When his sprain was well enough he rode out on horseback a good deal and often did not come back until late at night.

Then one afternoon he chanced to meet me and Adèle in the grounds; and while she played with Pilot he asked me to walk up and down a long beech avenue within sight of her. He then told me that she was the daughter of a French opera-dancer, Céline Varens, with whom he had once been in love. He had taken care of the child ever since her mother had died.

I thought better of him for that. Indeed, in the days that followed he seemed to change. He always had a word and a smile for me and, on several occasions, I read to him, or we talked together for hours at a time in the evenings. I began to feel as if he were my brother, rather than my master. I was happy. I came to think that when Mr. Rochester smiled his face was the object I most liked to see; his presence in a room was more cheering than the brightest fire.

He was still moody. More than once I found him sitting in the library alone, with his head bent on his folded arms. I grieved for him and would have given anything to be able to help him.

I lay one night in bed, and could not sleep for thinking of him.

"Will he go away again soon?" I asked myself. "Mrs. Fairfax said that he never stayed here longer than a fortnight at a time, and now he has been here eight weeks. If he does go, the place will be joyless without him."

I hardly know whether I slept or not after this musing. At any rate I started wide awake on hearing a sound, a strange murmur, which came, I thought, from just above me. I wished I had kept my candle burning. The night was dark and I felt more than a little afraid. I sat up in bed, listening. The sound was hushed.

I tried again to sleep, but my heart beat anxiously. The clock far down in the hall struck two. And then I was chilled with fear. I heard a whisper of sound, as if fingers had swept over the panels of my door in groping a way along the dark gallery outside.

"Who is there?" I called.

There was no answer. All at once I remembered that it might be Pilot, who, when the kitchen door chanced to be left open, sometimes found his way to

Mr. Rochester's door. I had seen him lying outside it in the mornings. The idea calmed me and I lay down. The house was still and hushed. I began to feel drowsy, but it was not fated that I should sleep that night.

The silence was suddenly shattered by a demonic laugh, uttered, it seemed, at the keyhole of my door. The head of my bed was near the door, and I thought at first that the goblin-laugher stood at my bedside. I rose with fast-beating heart, looked all round and could see nothing. The sound came again, and I knew it came from behind the panels of my door.

"Who is there?" I called again.

Something gurgled and moaned. I heard steps moving up the gallery towards the door that led to the third storey staircase. I heard it open and close—then all was still.

"Was that Grace Poole, and is she possessed with a devil?" I wondered.

I could not stay there by myself in the dark. I must go to Mrs. Fairfax. I hurried on my frock and a shawl and opened the door with a trembling hand. I was surprised to see a candle burning outside. Then I realized that the air was dim and smoky; that there was a strong smell of burning.

Something creaked loudly. It was a door ajar, and that door was Mr. Rochester's. I looked towards his room. Blue wreaths of smoke were rushing from it in a cloud. I saw a sudden flicker of light. My heart gave a great bound. Mr. Rochester's room was on fire!

Chapter Nine

Miss Ingram

I thought no more of Grace Poole or the mad laughter that I had heard. In an instant I was within the chamber. Tongues of flame darted around the bed; the curtains were on fire. In the midst of smoke and blaze Mr. Rochester lay stretched in deep sleep.

"Wake!" I cried. "Wake up!"

I shook him, but he only murmured and turned. The smoke had stupefied him. Not a moment could be lost: the very sheets were burning. I rushed to his water-basin and jug. Both were filled with water. I heaved them up and threw them over bed and man, flew back to my own room, brought my own water-jug and basin, and drenched the bed afresh.

Mr. Rochester was stirring at last. Though it was now dark, I knew he was awake, because I could hear him swearing at finding himself lying in a pool of water.

"Is there a flood?" he cried.

"No, sir," I answered, "but there has been a fire. Do please get up. I will fetch you a candle."

"In the name of all the elves, is that Jane Eyre?" he demanded. "What have you done, witch? Have you plotted to drown me?"

"In Heaven's name, get up!" I cried. "Indeed

somebody has plotted something. You cannot too soon find out who and what it is."

"Ah, here is my dressing-gown. Now run and fetch a candle."

I did run. I brought back the candle which still remained in the gallery. He took it from my hand, held it up, and looked at the bed, blackened and scorched, the sheets drenched, the carpet all round swimming in water.

"What is it? And who did it?" he asked.

I told him what I knew. He listened very gravely.

"Shall I call Mrs. Fairfax?" I asked, when I had told my story.

"No. What can she do? Take my cloak and wrap it round you. I am going to leave you for a few minutes. I shall take the candle. Stay where you are, and be as still as a mouse. Don't move, remember, or call anyone."

He went. I watched the light withdraw. He passed up the gallery very softly, unclosed the staircase door, and shut it after him. I was left in darkness. A very long time passed. I was about to move, when the light once more gleamed on the gallery wall. He re-entered, pale and very gloomy.

"It's as I thought," he said, putting his candle down on the washstand.

"How, sir?"

"You say that you heard an odd laugh?" he asked, frowning.

"Yes, sir. There is a woman who sews here, called Grace Poole—she laughs in that way. She is an odd person."

"Just so. Grace Poole—you have guessed it. She is, as you say, strange—very. However, say nothing about it. I'll sleep on the sofa in the library for the rest of the night. It's nearly four o'clock."

I made a move.

"Goodnight, sir," I said.

"What!" he exclaimed, "are you leaving me in that way? Why, you have saved my life—and you walk past me as if we were strangers! At least shake hands."

He held out his hand; I gave him mine: he took it first in one, then in both his own.

"Jane, you have saved my life," he said. "I am very much in your debt."

"There is no debt, sir," I answered. "Goodnight again."

"Wait," he said, still holding my hands. "I knew you would do me good in some way, when I first set eyes on you. I read it in your eyes—and your smile."

"I am glad I happened to be awake," I said; and then I was going.

"What! You will go?"

"I am cold, sir."

"Cold? Yes, and standing in a pool! Go then, Jane, go!" But he still held one hand, and I could not free it.

"I think I hear Mrs. Fairfax moving," I said hastily.

He let go of my hand, and I was gone. I went back to my bed, but never thought of sleep. I was too feverish to rest, and rose at dawn.

The morning passed as usual. I saw nothing of Mr. Rochester, but soon after breakfast I heard some bustle near his room. Mrs. Fairfax's voice, and Leah's, and the cook's—and even John's gruff tones. There were exclamations of "What a mercy master wasn't burnt in his bed!" "It's always dangerous to keep a candle lit at night!" and so on.

When dusk closed down, I had not heard Mr. Rochester's voice or step in the house all day. Surely, I thought, I shall see him before night. Darkness came in through the window and I went down to Mrs. Fairfax's room for tea. She looked at me, frowning a little.

"I am afraid you are not well today," she said. "You look flushed, and you ate so little dinner."

"Oh, I'm quite well," I said hurriedly.

She rose to draw the blind.

"Mr. Rochester has had a fine day for his journey," she remarked.

"Journey! Has Mr. Rochester gone away?"

"He went just after breakfast—to stay at 'The Leas', Mr. Eshton's place, ten miles on the other side of Millcote. I believe there is quite a party there."

"Do you expect him back tonight?"

"No, nor tomorrow either. I think he's likely to stay a week or more. He's a great favourite with the gentlemen of these parts; and the ladies are very fond of him, also."

"Are there ladies at 'The Leas'?"

"Oh, yes, it will be a large party. And the Honourable Blanche Ingram will be there. She is quite the most beautiful woman in the country."

"Is she—is she married?"

"No, but she is so beautiful that it cannot be long

before some gentleman takes a fancy to her. But you eat nothing, Miss Eyre! Are you ill?"

"No, I am too thirsty to eat. Will you let me have another cup?"

When I was alone once more, I thought over all that Mrs. Fairfax had said, and I knew that a greater fool than Jane Eyre had never lived. I realized that it is a madness in all women to let a secret love kindle within them. When Mr. Rochester had such a lovely creature as Blanche Ingram before his eyes, how could I imagine that he would think well of me?

My heart that night was heavy.

Two weeks later the post brought Mrs. Fairfax a letter while we were at breakfast.

"It's from the master," she said, and broke the seal.

I put down my coffee cup before she noticed that my hand had begun to shake. I waited while she read the letter.

"Mr. Rochester is not likely to return soon?" I asked, and I tried to keep my voice from shaking.

"Indeed, he is," cried Mrs. Fairfax. "In three days, he says; that will be next Thursday. And all the fine people at 'The Leas' are coming here to stay. All the best bedrooms are to be made ready—and Miss Ingram and the other ladies will bring their maids."

Miss Ingram! She was coming here! Was it not likely, I thought with sinking heart, that soon she would be Mrs. Rochester—and mistress of Thornfield Hall?

Chapter Ten

A Shriek in the Night

"Here he is!" said Mrs. Fairfax.

She stood at the schoolroom window, dressed in her best black satin gown. Adèle flew to her side. I followed, taking care to stand on one side so that I could see without being seen.

Four horses were galloping up the drive, and after them came two open carriages. Two of the horse-riders were young, dashing-looking gentlemen; the third was Mr. Rochester, with Pilot bounding before him, and at his side rode a lady in a purple riding-habit. Her veil streamed on the breeze and through its folds shone rich dark ringlets.

"Miss Ingram!" exclaimed Mrs. Fairfax, and away she hurried to receive the company.

Voices were now heard in the hall: gentlemen's deep tones and ladies' silvery accents blending together. The light steps came up the stairs; and there was a tripping through the gallery, and soft, cheerful laughs, and opening and closing doors, and, for a time, a hush.

"The ladies are changing their dresses," said Adèle. "Do you think Mr. Rochester will send for us after dinner?"

"No, indeed I don't. Mr. Rochester has something else to think about. Perhaps you'll see him tomorrow. Now, I must get your dinner."

We saw nothing of Mr. Rochester or his guests that night. The next day was fine and warm and the whole party rode out in the morning, some on horseback, some in the carriages. Mr. Rochester and Miss Ingram rode a little apart from the rest. When they had gone, Mrs. Fairfax brought me a message.

"Mr. Rochester would like Miss Eyre to bring Adèle down to the drawing-room after dinner."

When the time came I put on my best dress (the silver-grey one, bought for Miss Temple's wedding, and never worn since) along with my pearl brooch. We went downstairs.

There were eight ladies in the drawing-room, all very fine and tall. I curtseyed to them. One or two bent their heads in return, the others only stared at me. Blanche Ingram was straight and tall, and beautiful in a majestic way. Mr. Rochester was at her side, smiling into her eyes. Adèle was introduced to the ladies. I sat alone in a corner. The ladies and gentlemen talked and laughed together and I was ignored. At last Miss Ingram went to the piano and sang to her own accompaniment.

"Now is my time to slip away," I thought, when her song was done.

I left my corner and slipped through a side door which was near. A narrow passage led into the hall. In crossing it, I saw that my sandal was loose, and I knelt to tie it on the mat at the foot of the staircase. I heard the dining-room door open; I rose hastily; it was Mr. Rochester.

"How are you, Jane?" he asked.

"I am very well, sir."

"Why did you not come and speak to me in the room?"

"I did not wish to disturb you."

"You are a good deal paler than you were. What is the matter?"

"Nothing at all, sir."

"Come back to the drawing-room."

"I am tired, sir."

He looked at me for a minute.

"And a little sad," he said. "What about? Tell me, Jane."

"Nothing—nothing, sir. I am not sad."

"I say that you are. If I had time, I would know what all this means. Well, tonight I excuse you, but understand that so long as my visitors stay, I expect you in the drawing-room every evening. That is my wish. Now go, and send Sophie for Adèle. Goodnight, my—" He stopped, bit his lip, and left me. I went slowly to bed.

Thornfield was a merry and busy house during the next week. During this time, Mr. Rochester paid little regard to me—not that I could unlove him now, because he ceased to notice me, because I saw all his attention given to a great lady who scorned to touch me with the hem of her robe as she passed. She, I was sure, would be his future bride.

Then, one wet afternoon, Mr. Rochester was called to Millcote on business. At dusk a crunching of wheels and a splashing tramp of horse hoofs were heard on the wet gravel of the drive. A post-chaise was approaching. The door bell rang, and voices were heard in the hall. A moment later the newcomer was shown into the drawing-room. He bowed to Lady Ingram, who was there, as if he thought her the eldest lady present.

"It seems that I come at the wrong time, madam," he said, "when my friend, Mr. Rochester, is from home; but I arrive from a very long journey, and I am sure that he will not mind my waiting until he returns."

He was a tall man with a dark skin. There was something about him that was not altogether English. It was his voice, I decided, after the dressing bell had broken up the party.

When we gathered in the drawing-room that evening I learned that the newcomer was called Mason; that he had just arrived in England; and that he came from Jamaica, in the West Indies. I knew Mr. Rochester had been a traveller, and I guessed that it was in Jamaica that he had met the newcomer. We were all waiting for Mr. Rochester to return from Millcote and, as it happened, I met him in the hall when he did so. He greeted me with a smile.

"Sir," I said, "a stranger has arrived here since you left. He said that he was an old friend."

"The devil he did! Did he give his name?"

"His name is Mason, sir, and he comes from the West Indies."

Mr. Rochester took my hand and gripped it hard. The smile on his lips froze.

"Mason! The West Indies!" he said, and repeated the words again, his face turning whiter than ashes. He hardly seemed to know what he was doing. He sat down, and made me sit beside him. He took my hand and looked into my eyes.

"Jane," he said, "I wish I were on a quiet island with only you. Fetch me now a glass of wine from the dining-room; they will be at supper there; and tell me if Mason is with them. I'm going into the library."

I went. I found all the party at supper, which was arranged on the sideboard, and they stood about here and there in groups, their plates and glasses in their hands. Mr. Mason stood near the fire, talking to Colonel Dent. I filled a wine-glass and returned to the library. Mr. Rochester took the glass from my hand.

"What's Mason doing, Jane?" he asked.

"Laughing and talking, sir."

"Go back now into the room," he said. "Step quietly up to Mason and whisper in his ear that Mr. Rochester wishes to see him. Show him in here, and then leave us."

I did as he had asked. I ushered Mr. Mason into the library and then I went upstairs. At a late hour, after I had been in bed some time, I heard the visitors go to their rooms. I made out Mr. Rochester's voice and heard him say: "This way, Mason. This is your room."

He spoke cheerfully: the light tones set my heart at rest. I was soon asleep.

I had forgotten to draw my curtain, and when the moon rose, full and bright, its light roused me from sleep. Awaking in the dead of night, I opened my eyes on her silver-white disc. I half rose and stretched my arm to draw the curtain.

Heavens! What a cry!

The silence of the night was ripped apart by a fearful shriek. It ran from end to end of Thornfield Hall. My heart stood still; my stretched arm froze. The cry died, and sounded no more.

It had come out of the third storey. And now, overhead—yes, in the room just above my own—I heard the sounds of a struggle: a deadly one it seemed from the noise. A half-smothered voice shouted: "Help! Help! Help!" three times rapidly. And then: "Rochester! For God's sake, come!"

I heard a door open. Someone rushed along the gallery. Another step stamped on the flooring above and something fell; and there was silence.

I pulled on some clothes, though horror shook all my limbs. Everyone, it seemed, was awake. I went out into the gallery. Door after door opened. The gallery filled with ladies and gentlemen. "What is it?"—"What has happened?"—"Are there robbers?"—"Where shall we run?" was asked on every side.

"Where the devil is Rochester?" cried Colonel Dent. "I can't find him in his bed."

"Here! Here!" came a shout. "Calm yourselves! I'm coming now!"

The door at the end of the gallery opened. Mr. Rochester appeared with a candle.

"It's all right!" he cried, and his black eyes darted

sparks in the candlelight. "A servant has had a nightmare, that is all. She's an excitable person, and has taken a fit with fright. Now then, I must see you all back into your rooms, for, till the house is settled, she cannot be looked after."

One by one they all went back into their rooms. I did the same, not, however, to go to bed. Instead, I dressed myself carefully. The sounds I had heard after the scream, and the words that had been uttered, had probably only been heard by me. I knew that it was not a servant's dream which had so struck horror through the house.

I sat a long time by the window, looking out over the silent grounds. It seemed to me that some other event must follow the strange cry, struggle, and call.

No, stillness returned. In an hour Thornfield Hall was as hushed as a desert. I thought I would lie on my bed, dressed as I was. I left the window and moved with little noise across the carpet. Then, as I stopped to take off my shoes, a cautious hand tapped low at my door.

Chapter Eleven

Teeth Marks

I glided towards the door.

"Am I wanted?" I asked.

"Yes. Come out quietly," said Mr. Rochester's voice.

I obeyed. Mr. Rochester stood in the gallery, holding a light.

"Have you a sponge in your room?" he asked in a whisper.

"Yes, sir."

"And salts—smelling salts?"

"Yes."

"Go back and fetch both."

I did so.

"Come this way," he said then. "Take your time, and make no noise."

He glided up the gallery, up the stairs, and stopped in the dark, low corridor of the fateful third storey. He held a key in his hand and, approaching one of the small, black doors, he put it in the lock. He paused and spoke to me again.

"You don't turn sick at the sight of blood?"

"I don't think so," I answered. "I have never been tried yet."

I felt a thrill as I spoke, but no coldness and no faintness.

"Give me your hand," he said. I put my hand into his. "Warm and steady," was his remark. He turned the key and opened the door.

I saw a room I remembered having seen before, on the day Mrs. Fairfax showed me over the house. It was hung with tapestry, but the tapestry was now looped up in one part and behind it was a door. The door was open; a light shone out of the room within. I heard a snarling, snatching sound, almost like a dog quarrelling. Mr. Rochester put down his candle and looked at me.

"Wait a minute," he said, and went to the inner room.

A shout of laughter greeted his entrance; noisy at first, and dying away in Grace Poole's own goblin ha! ha! She was there, then.

I thought I heard a low voice speak to him. He came out and closed the door behind him.

"Here, Jane!" he said, and I walked round the other side of a large bed which, with its drawn curtains, had hidden a large part of the room. A man sat on an easy chair near the bed-head, all dressed except for his coat. He was still; his head leant back; his eyes were closed. Mr. Rochester held the candle over him and I recognized in his pale, lifeless face the stranger, Mason. I saw too that his shirt on one side and one arm were almost soaked in blood.

"Hold the candle," said Mr. Rochester, and I took it. He fetched a basin of water from the washstand. "Hold that," said he.

I obeyed. He took the sponge, dipped it in, and moistened the corpse-like face; then asked for my smelling-bottle and held it under Mason's nostrils.

The stranger opened his eyes and groaned. Mr. Rochester opened the shirt of the wounded man, whose arm and shoulder were bandaged. He sponged away blood, trickling fast down.

"Is it—is it dangerous?" murmured Mr. Mason.

"Pooh! No, a mere scratch. You'll be able to be removed by morning, I hope. Jane!"

"Sir?"

"I shall have to leave you in this room with this gentleman for an hour or two. You will sponge the blood as I did when it returns. You will not speak to him for any reason whatsoever—and, Richard, it will be at the peril of your life if you speak to her."

Again the poor man groaned. Mr. Rochester put the now red sponge into my hand, and left the room. The key grated in the lock, and the sound of his steps died away.

Here then I was in the third storey, locked in one of its strange rooms; night around me; a pale and wounded man under my eyes and hands; a murderess hardly separated from me by a single door. The rest I could bear; but I shuddered at the thought of Grace Poole bursting out upon me.

The long, slow minutes passed, but all the night I heard only three sounds—a step creak, a renewal of the snarling noise, and a deep human groan.

My own thoughts worried me. What mystery was it

that broke out at Thornfield, now in fire and now in blood, at the deadest hours of night? And this man I bent over—what had made him come to this part of the house when he should have been asleep in bed? Why, too, had Mr. Rochester hidden him away with his wound?

The night lingered and lingered, while my bleeding patient drooped, moaned, sickened—and neither day nor help arrived. He looked so weak and lost I feared he was dying; and I might not even speak to him!

The candle burnt out as the first streak of grey light edged the window curtains. Presently I heard Pilot bark far below. In five minutes more, the key grated in the lock. Mr. Rochester entered, and with him the surgeon he had been to fetch.

"Now, Carter, be quick," he said. "You've got half an hour to dress the wound and get the patient downstairs."

He drew back the thick curtain. The surgeon bent over Mason and unfastened the bandages. He looked up at Mr. Rochester.

"The flesh on the shoulder is torn as well as cut," he said. "This wound was not done with a knife; there have been teeth here!"

"She bit me," murmured Mason, "when Rochester took the knife from her. Oh, it was frightful!" he added, shuddering.

"I warned you," was his friend's answer. "It was foolish of you to go near her alone. Now, Carter, hurry! The sun will soon rise, and I must have him off."

"I must see to this other wound in the arm," replied the surgeon. "She has had her teeth here, too, I think."

"She sucked the blood—said she'd drain my heart," said Mason.

I saw Mr. Rochester shudder.

"Be quiet, Richard," he said curtly.

At last the surgeon had finished. Mason was wrapped in Mr. Rochester's cloak, and I was sent down to open a side door of the house. All the yard was quiet; but the gates stood wide open and there was a coach, with horses ready harnessed, and driver seated on the box, standing outside. The gentlemen came out of the house and helped Mason into the coach. Carter got in with him.

"Take care of him," said Mr. Rochester, "and keep him at your house till he is quite well. I'll ride over in a day or so to see how he is getting on."

Carter nodded, and the coach drove off. Mr. Rochester turned to me.

"You've passed a strange night, Jane," he said. "You are quite pale. Don't you curse me for disturbing your rest?"

"Curse you? No, sir."

He took my hands in his.

"What cold fingers!" he said. "How can I thank you, Jane—?"

There came the sound of men's voices. He started and let go my hands.

"Bless me!" he said. "There's Colonel Dent and Lynn in the stables! Go in by the shrubbery, Jane."

As I went one way he went another, and I heard him in the yard saying cheerfully:

"Mason got the start of you all this morning. He was gone before sunrise. I got up at four to see him off."

Chapter Twelve

A Summer's Night

All of Mr. Rochester's guests left Thornfield the next day. Once more, the weeks passed quietly and then, on Midsummer's Eve, the unexpected happened.

I was walking in the orchard by the light of the rising moon, and a nightingale was warbling in a wood. All was still and lovely, and then I heard a step. Mr. Rochester was coming towards me. I turned to walk back to the house.

"Jane," he called, "on so lovely a night it's a shame to sit in the house. Don't go. Walk with me."

I waited for him and we turned into the laurel walk.

"Jane," he said, "Thornfield is a pleasant place in summer, is it not?"

"Yes, sir."

"You must have grown to like the house—and be fond of Adèle and Mrs. Fairfax?"

"Yes, sir. I have an affection for them all."

"And would be sorry to part with them?"

"Yes."

"Pity!" he said, and sighed and paused. "It's a pity you must leave Thornfield."

My heart stood still.

"Must I?" I asked. "Must I leave Thornfield?"

"I'm sorry, but I really think you must, Jane."

This was a blow, but I tried not to show it.

"Well, sir," I said, "I shall be ready when the order to march comes."

"It is come now. I must give it tonight."

"Then you are going to be married, sir?"

"Exactly. You have hit the nail straight on the head."

"Soon, sir?"

"Very soon, my—that is, Miss Eyre. Adèle must go to school; and you must get a new situation."

"I'll advertise at once," I said, and my voice shook.

"I hope to marry in about a month," Mr. Rochester went on. "In the meantime I shall look out for a home for you."

"Thank you, sir."

"When friends are about to part, Jane, they like to spend the little time that remains to them close to each other. Come, let's sit here for half an hour, even though we may never do so again."

He led me towards a giant horse-chestnut that had a seat round its base. We sat down.

"Jane," he said, "do you hear that nightingale singing in the wood? Listen!"

In listening I let out a little sob. He stared at me.

"I wish I'd never come to Thornfield!" I exclaimed, in tears.

"Because you are sorry to leave it?" he asked.

"I love Thornfield," I cried, "but I see that I must go."

"Why?" he asked suddenly.

"Because Miss Ingram—your—bride—will not want me here."

"My bride! What bride? I have no bride!"

"But you will have."

"Yes—I will! I will!" He set his teeth as he spoke.

"Then I must go—you said it yourself."

"No! You must stay! I swear it—and the oath shall be kept."

"I tell you I must go!" I cried. "Do you think I can stay to become nothing to you? Do you think, because I am poor, that I have no heart?"

"No, Jane," he said quietly, taking me in his arms, pressing his lips on my lips. "I know that you have a heart."

"Let me go!" I cried.

I pulled myself away and stood before him. He looked up at me.

"Jane," he said, "I offer you my hand, my heart, and a share of all I own."

"You are joking with me!"

I cried.

"No, Jane," he answered, looking at me gently and seriously. "It is only you I intend to marry."

I was silent. I thought he mocked me.

"Come, Jane—come here."

"Your bride stands between us," I replied.

He rose, and with a stride reached me.

"My bride is here," he said, again drawing me to him. "Jane, will you marry me? Say yes, quickly."

"Mr. Rochester, let me look at your face. Turn to the moonlight."

He did so. I looked into his eyes and, in that moment, I saw that he meant what he said.

"Do you truly love me?" I asked. "Do you really wish me to be your wife?"

"I do. I swear it."

"Then, sir, I will marry you."

He gave a long, deep sigh, and we sat together on the bench. We stayed there a long time, while he spoke softly in my ear, his cheek laid on mine. And then, with a start, I realized that we were all in shadow. The moon was not yet set, but I could scarcely see my master's face, though I was sat close by him. The tree was writhing and groaning, while a wind roared in the laurel walk and came sweeping and gusting over us.

"There will be a storm," said Mr. Rochester. "We must go in."

"Tell me one thing," I said. "Why did you take such pains to make me think you wished to marry Miss Ingram when you had no intention of doing so?"

"Because I wished to make you as madly in love with me as I was with you, from the moment I first saw you in the lane. I knew that jealousy could best help me do that. Were you jealous, Jane?"

Before I could answer a livid, vivid spark leapt out of a cloud at which I was looking. There was a crack, a crash, and a close rattling of thunder. The rain rushed down. Mr. Rochester hurried me up the walk, through the grounds, and into the house; but we were quite wet before we entered the hall.

"Hasten to take off your wet things," he said. "And before you go, goodnight—goodnight, my darling!"

He kissed me, and then I ran upstairs.

Before I left my bed in the morning Adèle came running in to tell me that the great horse-chestnut at the bottom of the orchard had been struck by lightning in the night. It had been struck with such force that half of it had been split away.

Chapter 13

Wedding Day

A month passed, such a month of joy and happiness as I had never known. And then it was my wedding day.

Sophie came at seven to dress me. She took so long that Mr. Rochester sent up to ask why I did not come. "Jane!" I heard him call, and I hastened down. He met me at the foot of the stairs, and led me into the dining-room.

"I'll give you ten minutes to eat some breakfast," he said.

He rang the bell. A footman answered it.

"Is John getting the carriage ready?" asked Mr. Rochester.

"Yes, sir."

"Go to the church. See if Mr. Wood (the clergyman) is there and return and tell me."

The church was just beyond the gates; the footman soon returned.

"Mr. Wood is in the vestry, sir."

"And the carriage?"

"The horses are being harnessed."

"We shall not want it to go to church; but it must be ready the moment we return: all the boxes and luggage strapped on, and the coachman in his seat."

"Yes, sir."

"Jane, are you ready?"

I nodded and rose. There were no bridesmaids and no guests: none but Mr. Rochester and I. Mrs. Fairfax stood in the hall as we passed out.

Mr. Rochester paused at the churchyard gate. The grey old house of God rose calm before me. A rook was wheeling round the steeple, and the morning sky was red beyond. I noticed the figures of two strangers straying amongst the mossy headstones. Mr. Rochester led me up the path to the porch.

We entered the quiet church. The priest was waiting in his white surplice at the lowly altar, the clerk beside him. All was still: two shadows only moved in a far corner. The strangers had slipped in before us, and now stood with their backs to us, looking at an old tomb.

We took our place at the communion rail. I heard a quiet step behind me and glanced over my shoulder. One of the strangers was coming up the chancel. The service began; went on. At last the clergyman put out his hand to Mr. Rochester and asked: "Wilt thou have this woman for thy wedded wife?"

Before Mr. Rochester could answer, a near voice said:

"The marriage cannot go on. It must be stopped at once."

The clergyman looked up at the speaker, and stood mute. Mr. Rochester moved slightly, as if an earthquake had rolled under his feet, and then, without turning his head or eyes, he said: "Go on!"

There was a little silence. Mr. Rochester took my hand. The man who had spoken from behind us came forward and leaned on the rails.

"The marriage cannot go on," he said, calmly and steadily. "Mr. Rochester has a wife now living."

My nerves shook to those low-spoken words. I looked at Mr. Rochester. I made him look at me. His face was pale and as hard as rock. He twined my waist with his arm, and turned to the stranger.

"Who are you?" he asked.

"My name is Briggs. I am a solicitor, and my offices are in London."

"And you tell me that I already have a wife? Tell me also her name and where she lives."

"Certainly," said Mr. Briggs, and he calmly took a paper from his pocket.

"You were married fifteen years ago," he said, "to Bertha Antoinette Mason, at Jamaica, in the West Indies. I have a copy of the record of the marriage."

"That does not prove that my wife is still living."

"She was living three months ago," returned the solicitor.

"How do you know?"

"I have a witness to the fact."

"Produce him."

"I will—he is on the spot. Mr. Mason, have the goodness to step forward."

Mr. Rochester, on hearing the name, set his teeth. The second stranger, who had waited in the background, now drew near. Yes, it was Mason himself. Mr. Rochester turned and glared at him, and lifted his strong arm. Mason shrank away in fright.

"Well?" asked Mr. Rochester. "What have you to say?"

"Your wife is now living at Thornfield Hall," said Mason. "I saw her there last April." He turned to the clergyman. "I am her brother," he said.

"At Thornfield Hall!" exclaimed the clergyman. "Impossible! I never heard of a Mrs. Rochester at Thornfield."

I saw a grim smile twist Mr. Rochester's lips.

"No," he said, "I took care that none should hear of her under that name. Enough! Wood, take off your surplice. There will be no wedding today."

The man obeyed. Mr. Rochester went on.

"Gentlemen, I did not mean to do wrong. What this lawyer and his client say is true—the woman to whom I was married lives. You've never heard of a Mrs. Rochester, Wood; but I daresay you've heard the gossip about the mysterious lunatic at the Hall, who is kept under lock and key. I now tell you that she is my wife. Bertha Mason is mad, however, and she came of a mad family—something I found out only after we were married. Briggs, Wood, Mason—I invite you all to come up to the house and visit Mrs. Poole's patient. This girl," he went on, looking at me, "knew nothing of my disgusting secret. Come, all of you, follow!"

Still holding me fast, he left the church, the three gentlemen coming after. At the front door of the hall we found the carriage.

"Take it back to the coach-house, John," said Mr. Rochester coolly. "It will not be wanted today."

He passed into the house and went up the stairs, still holding my hand, and with the other gentlemen following. We mounted the first staircase, went on to the third storey. Mr. Rochester took out a key and opened a low, black door. We went into the tapestried room, with its great bed.

"You know this place, Mason," said our guide. "She bit and stabbed you here."

He lifted the hangings from the hall, uncovering the second door: this, too, he opened. In a room without a window there burnt a fire. Grace Poole bent over it, cooking something in a saucepan. In the deep shadow at the far end a figure ran backwards and forwards. It growled like some strange wild animal; but it was covered with clothing, and a wild mane of hair hid its head and face.

The creature suddenly gave a fierce cry.

"Sir! She sees you!" exclaimed Grace. "You'd better not stay. Take care, sir!"

The three gentlemen stepped back. Mr. Rochester flung me behind him. The lunatic sprang.

She was a big woman, and strong. He could have settled her with a blow, but he would not strike her. At last he mastered her arms. Grace Poole gave him a cord, and he tied them behind her. With more rope he bound her to a chair. She struggled all the time, and kept giving the fiercest yells. Mr. Rochester turned to the horrified watchers with a twisted smile.

"Gentlemen," he said, "that is my wife!"

Chapter Fourteen

Flight

Some time in the afternoon I raised my head and saw the western sun gilding the walls of my room. There I had lain since I left the room on the third floor, asking myself the same question over again and over again: "What am I to do?"

At last I made up my mind. I would leave Thornfield at once. I rose and stumbled to the door. I drew the bolt and passed out. I stumbled: my head was dizzy, my sight dim, and my limbs feeble. I fell, but not to the ground, for an outstretched arm caught me. I looked up—I was held by Mr. Rochester, who sat in a chair across the threshold of my room.

"I've been waiting for you," he said. "Jane, will you ever forgive me? I did not mean to hurt you!"

In my heart I forgave him at that moment, but not in words.

"I cannot," I said. "I am tired and sick. I want some water."

He lifted me in his arms and carried me downstairs. He put wine to my lips. I tasted it and felt better. I was in the library, sitting in his chair.

"Jane," he said, "I must tell you why I did this thing. You must know that my father was a greedy and grasping man. He wanted me to be provided for by a wealthy marriage and he sent me to the West Indies to meet an old friend of his, a Mr. Mason, who was a rich planter. Mason, he knew, had a son and daughter and he had learned that the daughter would receive thirty thousand pounds when she married. When I arrived in Jamaica I found that this Miss Mason was both young and beautiful. I often met her at parties, but seldom saw her alone, and had very little opportunity to speak privately with her. Her family wanted me to marry her and, mole-eyed blockhead that I was, I did so.

"My bride's mother I had never seen: I understood she was dead. Later, I learned that I was wrong: she was only mad, and shut up in a lunatic asylum. There was a younger brother, too, a dumb idiot; and the elder brother, whom you have seen, will probably be in the same state one day.

"As time passed, I began to find things out. My wife was both cruel and quarrelsome. Four years later my father died and left me a rich man—and at the same time the doctors discovered that my wife was mad. She had to be shut up, and my life became a misery. To Thornfield, then, I brought her. Only Grace Poole and Carter, the surgeon, have ever known who she was, though I think that Mrs. Fairfax may have suspected something.

"During these last ten years I roamed about the world, returning here only to make sure that my secret was safe. And then I found you. I thought you good, gifted, lovely, and I wanted to marry you. Jane, don't leave me now! Say that you return my love! Say it, Jane! Say it!"

A pause. It was a terrible moment, full of struggle, blackness, burning. No human being that ever lived could wish to be loved better than I was loved. I knew that, but I knew my duty, also. I rose and walked to the door.

"You are going, Jane?"

"Yes, I am going."

"Oh, Jane!" he cried. "My hope—my love —my life!"

Then came a deep, strong sob. I opened the door and went back to my own room.

I had no sleep that night. But July nights are short and at the coming of dawn I rose and dressed. All that I owned I made into a small parcel. My purse, holding twenty shillings, I put in my pocket. I tied on my straw bonnet, pinned my shawl, took the parcel, and stole from my room.

My heart stopped its beating at the threshold of Mr. Rochester's room and my foot was forced to stop also. He was not sleeping. He was walking restlessly from wall to wall. He was waiting for the morning when he would send for me. I should be gone.

Drearily I wound my way downstairs. I opened the door, passed out, shut it softly. Dim dawn glimmered in the yard. The gates were closed and locked, but a wicket in one of them was only latched. Through that I departed.

I do not know for how many hours I walked that summer's day. I went on and on, following a road that

I did not know, until at last I was forced to rest under the hedge that ran beside it.

Minutes later I heard wheels, and saw a coach come on. I stood up and lifted my hand. It stopped. I asked where it was going. The driver named a place a long way off. I asked for what sum he would take me there and was told thirty shillings. I answered I had but twenty. Well, he would try to make it do. I entered the coach, was shut in, and it rolled on its way.

I sat there while my heart broke, and the tears poured from my eyes.

Chapter Fifteen

Discovery

It was a summer evening, two days later. The coachman had set me down at a place called Whitcross—a stone pillar set up where four roads met. He could take me no further for the sum I had given him.

There were great moors behind and on each hand of me, and waves of mountains far beyond. What was I to do? Where to go? I had no answer. I struck straight across the moor.

That evening I ate berries and slept in the heather with my shawl spread over me. When I walked on next morning, I followed a road that brought me into a village. In its one street there was a little shop with bread in the window.

I entered the shop. A woman was there.

"Please," I said, "will you give me a roll for this handkerchief?"

She frowned at me and shook her head.

"Nay," she said, "I never sell stuff that way."

"Will you take my gloves?"

"No! What could I do with them?"

I turned away and walked on, out of the village and along the track that led over the moor. That night I slept in a wood. Towards morning it rained, and the whole of the next day was wet. As dusk came down I saw a trace of white over the moor. It was a path that led up to a big house, standing behind a low stone wall. A light shone from one window. I groped my way round to the back door. I knocked. The door opened and a woman looked out.

"What do you want?" she asked.

"I want a night's shelter in an outhouse, and a crust of bread to eat."

A look of distrust showed on the woman's face.

"If you're a friend of thieves who are hanging about nearby," she said, "you can tell them we've got dogs and a gun in the house."

With that she slammed the door.

I was starving and quite worn out; not another step could I stir. I sank down on the wet doorstep and wept. A minute later a dark form walked towards me out of the gloom.

"Why!" said a man's voice. "What have we here?" and, with a loud, long knock, the newcomer rapped several times on the door.

"Is it you, Mr. St. John?" cried a voice within.

"Yes. Open quickly."

The door opened. A few minutes later I stood, sick and trembling, within a bright, clean kitchen. Two young ladies, their brother Mr. St. John, and the old servant, were all gazing at me. My head swam; I felt myself falling; I knew no more.

I learned later that I was unconscious for three days and nights, during which time the two young ladies nursed me. I woke at last in a small room. On a chair by the bedside were all my own things, clean and dry.

Two days later I was able to get up, and Mr. St. John Rivers, the clergyman to whom the house belonged, came to visit me. I told him a little of my story—about my days at Lowood, that I had been a governess, and so on. My name, I thought it best to add, was Jane Elliott.

During the next few days my health improved so much that I could sit up all day and walk out sometimes. The days passed and Mr. St. John and his sisters said nothing of my leaving them. One morning, however, the clergyman called me into his study.

"Miss Elliott," he said, "I want to help you if I can. We are planning to open a girls' school at Morton, the nearest village, and we should like you to become its mistress. A cottage of two rooms is attached to the school for the mistress, and her salary will be thirty pounds a year. The job is yours if you wish."

"Thank you," I said. "I accept with all my heart."

A week later I moved into my new home—a little cottage with white-washed walls and a sanded floor. I had twenty pupils and spent my days in a bare and humble schoolroom.

The weeks and months passed. It was hard work at first, but it kept my mind busy and I felt I became a favourite in the neighbourhood. Whenever I went out I was welcomed with friendly smiles. I saw a lot of Mr. Rivers and his sisters, who became my very good friends.

Winter came again, bringing days of keen winds and blinding falls of snow. I sat one stormy evening, reading by my fire, when the latch rattled and St. John

Rivers came in out of the howling darkness, his cloak all white as a glacier. He was the last person I had expected to see on such a night.

"Why are you come?" I asked. "Has anything happened?"

He stamped the snow from his boots, took off his cloak and hung it up. He sat down, taking out a pocket-book and, from it, a letter.

"I want to tell you a story," he said. "Some of it you may have heard before, and you may be able to add things that I don't yet know. I shan't keep you very long. This is it:

"Twenty years ago a poor curate fell in love with a rich man's daughter. She fell in love with him and married him, against the advice of her family, who at once disowned her. Before two years had passed the rash pair were both dead, and laid quietly side by side in one grave. They left a daughter who was taken in and reared by an aunt, called Mrs. Reed, of Gateshead—you start—did you hear a noise? Mrs. Reed kept the orphan ten years and then sent the girl to Lowood School, where you stayed so long yourself. From a pupil she became a teacher, like yourself. She left Lowood to become a governess, like yourself, at the home of a certain Mr. Rochester."

"Mr. Rivers!" I interrupted.

"I can guess your feelings," he said, "but hear me to the end. I know nothing of Mr. Rochester except that he offered to marry this young girl, and that at the very altar she discovered that he had a wife yet alive, though a lunatic. The girl left Thornfield Hall in the night and vanished. It is now become urgent that she should be found. I have myself received a letter from a Mr. Briggs, a solicitor, telling me the story. Is it not an odd tale?"

"Just tell me this," I said, "what of Mr. Rochester? How and where is he? What is he doing? Is he well?"

"I don't know. He must have been a bad man," said Mr. Rivers.

"He was not! You don't know him!" I cried.

He sighed.

"Briggs wrote to me of a Jane Eyre," he said. "I knew at once that it was you. You do own the name, don't you?"

"Yes," I answered. "But what did Mr. Briggs want with me?"

"To tell you that your uncle, Mr. Eyre, of Madeira, is dead: that he has left you all his property, and that you are now rich."

"I! Rich?"

"Yes. He has left you some twenty thousand pounds."

The news took away my breath. St. John Rivers smiled and rose to his feet.

"Stop one minute!" I cried. "It puzzles me to know why Mr. Briggs wrote to you about me."

He stood still and silent a moment, then smiled again.

"My mother's name," he said, "was Eyre. She had two brothers: one a clergyman who married Miss Jane Reed of Gateshead; the other John Eyre, a merchant of Madeira. Mr. Briggs, being Mr. Eyre's solicitor, wrote to us last August to tell us of our uncle's death; and to say that he had left his fortune to his brother the clergyman's orphan daughter. He wrote again a few days back to say that the heiress was lost, and asking if we knew anything of her. The rest you know."

I stood up.

"Your mother was my father's sister?"

"Yes."

"Then you and your sisters are my cousins?"

He bowed.

"We are cousins, yes."

I clapped my hands in sudden joy.

"Oh! I am glad!" I cried. "Tell your sisters that I will share my fortune with you all. I will come and live with the three of you at Moor House. I never had a home, but I must and will have one now."

"And the school, Miss Eyre?" he asked.

"I will keep my post till you find someone to take my place."

He smiled again. We shook hands and he left me.

A few weeks later I moved into Moor House to live with my cousins, to each of whom I had given five thousand pounds.

Chapter Sixteen

Ferndean

May had come round again. For some months I had been happy. I had a home, I had friends, I was, to a point, content. But I could not forget Mr. Rochester, not for a moment. His idea was still with me, and nothing could wash it away.

I had written to Mrs. Fairfax, asking her for news of him. I was astonished when a fortnight passed away without reply; but when the months wore away, and day after day the post arrived and brought nothing for me, I was really anxious.

I wrote again. Half a year passed and no reply. Then, indeed, my hope died out and it was as if something precious had gone out of my life.

A fine spring shone round me which I could not enjoy. And then there came that evening in May when, at bed-time, his sisters and I stood round St. John Rivers and wished him good-night. He kissed his sisters and gave me his hand. Diana, the youngest, exclaimed:

"St. John! You call Jane your third sister, but you don't kiss her also."

She pushed me towards him, and the two of them ran from the room. St. John looked at me out of his deep blue eyes.

"Wait, Jane," he said quietly. "Don't go to bed yet.

There is something I must say to you. In six weeks I am going to India. You know that I have always wanted to do missionary work and now it is all arranged. Jane, will you marry me, and come with me as my wife?"

There was a little silence. I thought over what he had said. All the house was still. The one candle was dying out, the room was full of moonlight. My heart beat fast and thick: I heard its throb. Suddenly it stood still. I seemed to hear a voice, far off, calling to me.

"Jane! Jane! Jane!"—nothing more.

"I am coming!" I cried. "Wait for me!"

I flew to the door and looked into the passage: it was dark. I ran out into the garden: it was empty.

"Where are you?" I cried.

There was only the wind sighing low in the firs. All else was moorland, loneliness and hush.

I broke from St. John, who had followed me, ran into the house and up to my room. I locked myself in and lay down. I knew what I must do and I was eager for daylight to come.

I rose early. It was a Tuesday, and the first of June. At breakfast I told Diana and Mary that I was going on a journey and should be away at least four days.

Early that afternoon I stood at the foot of the sign-post of Whitcross, waiting for the coach that was to take me to distant Thornfield.

It was a journey of six-and-thirty hours. On the Thursday morning the coach stopped to water the horses at a wayside inn. On its sign I read in gilt letters, "The Rochester Arms". My heart leapt up. I was already on my master's lands. I paid my fare and gave my trunk into the ostler's charge, to be kept till I called for it.

There was a stile before me. Almost before I knew what I was doing I was crossing the fields. How fast I walked! How I ran sometimes! How I looked forward to catching my first sight of the house!

I walked along the wall of the orchard. There was a gate just there, between two stone pillars, crowned by stone balls. I peeped around a pillar. I looked with joy towards the stately house: I saw a blackened ruin.

The lawn, the grounds, were trodden and waste. The front was no more than a shell-like wall, very high, and with paneless windows. No roof, no battlements, no chimneys—all had crashed in. And there was the silence of death about it. The grim blackness of the stones told by what fate the Hall had fallen—by fire! But how? What had happened to Mr. Rochester? Was he dead?

I had to know the answer. I turned and ran back to the inn. I called for the landlord.

"You know Thornfield Hall?" I asked.

"Yes, ma'am. It's a ruin. It was burnt down about last harvest-time. The fire broke out at dead of night. It was a terrible sight. I saw it myself."

"How did it start?" I asked faintly.

"There was a lady—a lunatic—kept in the house. She set it going. She got out of her room one night and set fire to the hangings in the room next door. Then she went on, from room to room, till all of the top floor was well ablaze. Mr. Rochester was not sleeping well that night, and he was the first to give the alarm. He got all the servants out of their beds and then went back to fetch his mad wife out of the flaming building. She'd got out onto the roof and there she stood, waving her arms and shouting out till they could hear her a mile off. I saw her with my own eyes. I saw Mr. Rochester come out through the skylight onto the roof. He went towards her; and then, ma'am, she yelled and gave a spring, and the next minute she lay smashed on the ground."

"Dead?"

"Yes, dead." He shuddered. "It was frightful! Well, ma'am, the house was burnt to the ground."

"Were any other lives lost?"

"No—everyone was all right—except for poor Mr. Rochester."

My heart stopped. My blood ran cold.

"Is he—is he dead?" I gasped.

"No. He's in England now. He can't leave it, I fancy. He's stone-blind. As he came down the staircase there was a great crash—all fell. He was taken out from under the ruins alive—but a beam had knocked out one eye, and one hand was so crushed that it had to be taken off by the surgeon. He's blind, and a cripple."

"Where is he? Where does he live now?"

"At Ferndean—a house he has on a farm, about thirty miles off. Only his old coachman and his wife are with him now. He's quite broken down, they say."

"Get me a carriage!" I gasped. "If your post boy can

drive me to Ferndean before dark, I'll pay both you and him twice the amount you ask!"

They got me there just before dark. It was raining. Iron gates between granite pillars showed me where to enter, and passing through them I saw the house, with two pointed gables in its front. It was as still as a church on a weekday. I drew very near.

"Can there be life here?" I asked.

Yes, the front door was opening. A figure came out into the twilight. It was my master, Edward Rochester.

He moved slowly and gropingly forward. Then he paused, as if he did not know which way to turn, and stood quiet in the rain, now falling fast on his uncovered head. At this moment John, the old coachman, came round the side of the house.

"Will you take my arm, sir?" he said. "You'd better go in."

"Let me alone," was the answer.

John withdrew, without having seen me. Mr. Rochester stood there some minutes longer, then groped his way back to the house. The front door closed behind him.

I now drew near and knocked. John's wife opened the door for me. She started as if she had seen a ghost.

"Is it really you, miss?" she said, a hand on her heart.

She took me by the hand and led me into the kitchen, where John now sat by a good fire. I asked him to go down to the inn and bring back my trunk. A minute later the parlour bell rang. Mary picked up a tea-tray.

"Is that what he rang for?" I asked.

"Yes, and he always has candles brought in at dark, though he is blind."

"Give the tray to me. I will carry it in."

I took it from her hands. She pointed to me the parlour door. The tray shook as I held it. My heart struck my ribs loud and fast. Mary opened the door and shut it behind me.

He was standing before the fire. His old dog, Pilot, lay on one side. Pilot pricked up his ears when I came in. Then he jumped up with a yelp and bounded towards me. He almost knocked the tray from my hands. I set it on the table, then patted him, and said softly, "Lie down!"

I moved towards Mr. Rochester. Pilot followed me, still excited. I saw Mr. Rochester frown.

"What's the matter, Pilot?" he asked.

"Down, Pilot!" I said again.

Mr. Rochester seemed to freeze.

"This is you, Mary, is it not?" he asked.

"Mary is in the kitchen," I answered.

He put out his hand and groped. I took his wandering hand, and held it in both mine.

"Her fingers!" he cried. "Jane! It is you!"

"Yes," I answered. "I came this evening."

He pulled me to him and held me close.

"My dear master," I said. "I have found you again—I have come back to you."

"Jane," he said, "I am blind and crippled—"

I put my hand on his lips, then clung closer to him.

"It makes no difference," I said.

"Jane," he said, "a poor blind man asks you to marry him. Will you, Jane?"

"Yes, sir," I said.

"Last Monday night," he said quietly, "between eleven and twelve o'clock, I was sitting by the open window of my room. I longed for you, Jane! I could not help myself—I called your name aloud: 'Jane! Jane! Jane!' A voice—your voice—answered me: 'I am coming! Wait for me'; and a moment after went whispering on the wind the words: 'Where are you?' In spirit I believe we must have met. I heard you, Jane, as certain as I live. And now you have come back to me!"

"Yes," I said. "I have come back to you—for ever!"

"I thank God!" he said. "Yes, I thank God!"

I took his dear hand and held it to my lips, then let it pass round my shoulder. I was so much smaller than he, but I knew that from that day I should serve as his prop and guide.

I have now been married ten years, and no woman was ever happier than I am. Mr. Rochester was blind for the first two years of our marriage. Then, one morning, as I was writing a letter to his dictation, he came and bent over me and said:

"Jane, have you a glittering ornament round your neck?"

I had a gold watch-chain. I answered, "Yes."

"And have you a pale blue dress on?"

I had. He told me then that for some time he had thought that the cloud over his one eye was clearing, and that he was now sure of it. He and I went up to

London. He had the advice of a famous oculist, and in time recovered the sight of that one eye.

He cannot now see too well; he cannot read or write much; but he can find his way about without being led by the hand. The sky is no longer blank to him, the earth no longer empty. When our first son was put into his arms, he could see that the boy had his own eyes—large, brilliant, and black. And in his eye, then, I saw shining the light of his love for us both.

I am on. He breathed heavily. I sat there, scared, and the silence — dead silence of the one-roomed...

The cabman saw me until the sunlight would writh... doubt, but he had but was shop... out being hit a shop thing. The rat... and longer himself am... when... the person... when or either... it was out some... in some two that ... Ky... hin sit so eyes... he could... and blew... until the do that ... in time to help of... reste... to sub.

Glossary

The words and phrases in the glossary that follows have been chosen to help the reader understand their meaning in the specific context of this book (although sometimes they may have other additional meanings). Most of the words or phrases belong to the more formal language of the 19th century, much of which is no longer in regular use today. We recommend you also use a dictionary when reading this book.

abrupt talking to other people in a brief and unfriendly way

ale beer

battlements a wall about chest height round the roof of a large building, such as a castle, originally to help defend it from attack but later just for decoration

bewildered puzzled or confused

bewitch to cast a spell over someone or something

blockhead a very stupid person

Bluebeard a violent and bloodthirsty nobleman (a character in a French folk tale who murders his wives)

brooch a piece of jewellery that is pinned to a woman's dress or jacket

brows short for eyebrows

by-and-by soon or in a short while

carriage a horse-drawn vehicle

cautious careful especially when things are dangerous or uncertain

changeful often changing

chilblains swollen fingers or toes because of a long time spent in the cold

closed down fell or came down

consumption an old name for tuberculosis, an infectious disease caused by bacteria

crib a child's bed or cot

crimson deep red

curtesy a greeting made by women when they bend their knees and lower their heads slightly

dead silence complete silence or without any noise

demonic laugh maniacal laughter

Devil take me! an exclamation of surprise or anger

dormitory a large room containing a lot of beds, especially in a boarding school

drawing-room a room in a large house for relaxing or for entertaining guests

drearily sadly or in great misery

dressing bell a bell rung in the early evening to tell people it was time for them to go and get dressed for dinner—in Jane Eyre's time people changed from their day dress to a more formal dress for the evening meal

drew close closed

fairy tales children's stories about magical creatures like fairies and elves

felling knocking down

frock dress

gallery a long enclosed passage such as a corridor

gilding turning to gold

goblin a mythological ugly, magical being who likes to make trouble for human beings

governess a woman teacher employed privately to teach children in their homes

gown a woman's dress for formal events

hardy robust or sturdy or with a strong state of health

holding me fast holding me tightly or firmly

horse-chestnut a tree with white flowers and nutlike seeds

I shall do I shall manage or I shall be okay

keenly strongly or extremely coldly

lane a narrow road between buildings or hedges

lantern a light inside a protective case that can be carried

laurel walk a path in a garden meant for walking along, with sweet smelling laurel trees on either side

low quietly or softly

lunatic asylum (now an offensive term) a psychiatric hospital where insane people were kept

make haste hurry along

mansion a large and impressive house

mirthless without laughter or not cheerful

mole-eyed having poor eyesight or almost blind

moor a large area of open ground, usually having peaty soil and covered with heather, coarse grass, bracken and moss

musing thinking deeply about something

mute silent

my flesh shrank I became very frightened

oculist an old-fashioned word for a doctor who is specially trained to look after people's eyes—now known as an ophthalmologist or optometrist

of these parts in this area or neighbourhood

ostler a man who looks after horses especially at an inn

parlour a small living room

pinafore a sleeveless dress worn to keep the clothes underneath clean, or a kind of apron

pocket-book a small bag or case for money or papers that is carried in the pocket

porter a man in charge of a gate or door

portfolio a case or folder for holding drawings and paintings

post-chaise a closed, four-wheeled carriage pulled by horses

prop support

quilt a thick warm cover for a bed

ran his eye over looked carefully at

references a written letter praising a person's character and abilities (usually given to possible employer by an applicant for a job)

relish with enjoyment or liking

riding-habit a special garment worn by ladies for riding on horseback

ringlets locks of hair hanging down in spiral curls

rook a large black bird belonging to the crow family

scarce only just

scorching burning

sealed with fixed with a wax seal

short cut a way or route that is shorter than the usual way

situation a job or employment

slate a piece of slate for writing on (like a blackboard/chalkboard)

smelling salts a strong-smelling mixture that helps to revive people who have fainted or are unconscious

snuff to examine by sniffing

snug comfortable and warm

sponge a piece of the light porous highly absorbent elastic skeleton of certain sponges (an animal that lives in the sea) that is used in bathing, cleaning, etc.

spur a pointed device fixed to the heel of a riding boot that is used to make a horse run faster

spurred heel the heel of a riding boot that has spurs attached

stammer to speak in a hesitant way

started jumped suddenly

stile a set of steps in a wall or over a fence

stole from left quietly and secretly

storey a set of rooms at one level of a building

stupefied dazed

stupefy to cause someone to be unable to think clearly

surgeon a doctor who does medical operations

take great pains to make a lot of effort to do something properly or to try very hard

tapestry a heavy cloth, hand-sewn with a picture that is used to decorate walls

thrill of grief a strong feeling of sadness

to be obliged to someone to be grateful to someone or to say thank you to someone

to speak between one's teeth to speak with a clenched jaw in anger or irritation

to take a fancy to to be attracted to someone or something

topknot long hair arranged on top of the head

totter to shake or sway

trap-door a small door in the ceiling of a room

typhus a disease caused by a bacteria found on head lice

usher to show someone into a room in a polite and kindly way

veil a piece of almost see-through material usually attached to a hat or a headdress, as in a wedding veil

waned faded

wicket short for "wicket gate", a small gate or door that is part of a larger gate or door

with some stress quite heavily or with some force

wreaths of smoke a drifting mass of smoke